ROSE

WIL

CW00408429

Will Parfitt

Will has been a writer since receiving his first typewriter when he was 12 years old and is the author of several non-fiction psychology and Kabbalah books, the most recent being *The Magic of Psychosynthesis* (2019). His fiction books include *This Beautiful Earth* (2016) and *Meetings with Amazing People* (2017). Will lives in Glastonbury, England, and can be contacted via his website:

www.willparfitt.com

To Melanie
with love from
Will 08/22

other books currently available
by the same author

FICTION
Meetings with Amazing People
The Great Circle of Time
This Beautiful Garden

KABBALAH
The Complete Guide to the Kabbalah
Kabbalah: The Tree of Life
Kabbalah For Life

PSYCHOLOGY
The Magic of Psychosynthesis
The Something and Nothing of Death
Psychosynthesis: The Elements and Beyond
Walking Through Walls
The Elements of Psychosynthesis
Psychosynthesis: Beyond the Elements

Rose of Heaven

and other stories

WILL PARFITT

PSA BOOKS

Glastonbury, England

© Will Parfitt

First published in the U.K. in 2022 by PSA Books

PSA Books
27, BA6 8AB, U.K.
www.willparfitt.com

Will Parfitt asserts the moral right
to be identified as the author of this work.

All the characters in these stories
are a product of the author's imagination
and any resemblance to actual people
is purely coincidental.

Design: Will Parfitt

ISBN 978-1-9999763-2-3

Contents

Rose of Heaven 6

Nothing Like a Hole in the Head 30

The Return of Nikodemos 39

Whatever Happened to Saul, Paul
 David and Catherine? 54

Surrender 68

Not All Here 80

The Wisdom of the Birds 85

Mabel's Mindfulness 90

The Magician's House 108

Rose of Heaven

I first met her when I was twelve years old. I had no idea it was to be a special day, the most special ever for a twelve year old boy. So far it was typical; a dull day in the long summer vacation. I moseyed about the house, and was now sauntering down the garden path. Kicking open the garage door, I peered inside where my father's car usually sat, the empty space soiled with oil drips and smelling vaguely of car. I didn't enter. I looked down at the night-scented stock my gran had encouraged me to plant, and wondered, yet again, when it would start smelling at night. I picked up a stick, waved it in the air, and idly dropped it again. I was hoping there was a friend or two to play with in the back lane, but somehow I expected it to be empty. It was one of those days. I shuffled my feet and approached the back gate.

As soon as I opened the gate she looked up. We faced one another, eye to eye, for a few seconds only. I'd never seen her before yet I felt I knew her better than I knew myself. My heart exploded. My whole being was reaching out to touch the girl standing there. A few seconds only, but they lasted a very long time. I drank her in, all of her body, her being, entwining with mine. We became one being. I felt I'd know her for a long, long time. I melted and she melted, losing an old innocence and, at the same time, nourished by a new innocence.

I was face to face with the most beautiful girl – person – I had ever seen in my life. About my age, short, thin, and with a cascade of dark curls round a tanned face. Or was it even a dirty face? Her large black eyes reflected depths inside me that I'd never encountered, not even in my deepest, darkest dreams. Her eyes reflected mine, my eyes reflected hers, and we were lost in a strange, entrancing oneness.

I knew I wanted her forever: my twin, my sister, my partner, my lover; concepts beyond my twelve-year-old's recognition flooded my being. I don't believe I had time to feel sexual, but I felt an identity between her body and mine that was instantly recognisable. I knew I didn't imagine it and I knew she felt it too. Whilst trapped in the depths of her eyes, I took in the rest of the vision. Although her dress was drab, to me she was shining. Everything else in the world held even less interest than before. She stood out, her small body rippling with energy and shaking. Even her brown, dirty knees, looked smooth and enticing.

Almost as if that moment had never happened, all too quickly she broke the gaze. Panic swelling up to cloud her vision and block mine, she turned and started running from me. I tried to call out, "Wait!" but the word choked in my throat. I don't think any sound actually came but I was crying out inside, imploring her not to run. My body was frozen. My throat was frozen.

She was running now, down the lane, round the corner. Somehow, I couldn't run after her, I couldn't follow. Feeling shaken to my core, I felt separated from myself, let alone from her. I fought my way through a thick fog, a deep gooey slime of unknowing, and somehow made it to my bedroom. Throwing myself onto my bed, I sobbed. And sobbed. I felt a rising throbbing, incongruent with my sobbing yet somehow inextricably linked with it; a rising, hardening and familiar throbbing in my penis, but this was different. I didn't want to masturbate it away, it filled my body with thrilling, painfully thrilling waves of longing.

I knew exactly who she was. A poor, little urchin who'd been going through the dustbin outside our back gate. Startled at being discovered, she quickly panicked and ran, shamed. A little girl caught in an act that somehow, somewhere she had learned to do, but do with shame. A little girl, yes, but also a woman who somehow touched my depths and who married my soul in that brief encounter.

I had fantasies about finding her caravan and rescuing her, for I was sure, in my naivety, that she lived in a van and therefore needed rescuing. Anyone who had to go through dustbins needed a knight in shining armour to come and take them away from their poverty and disgrace. With a new stiffness in my back, and a heroic gaze, I tried telling mum and dad, wanting to enlist their aid in my quest. Their knowing glances to one another embarrassed me and I never mentioned her to them again. I wandered the streets hoping to bump into her. Every time I opened the back gate, especially on bin day, my heart leapt into my throat on realising she might be there. And I always knew she wouldn't be. I knew she had gone. I also knew that I would find her, but only when the time was right.

How I yearned for that time to come.

The Train

She entered the railway carriage and sat opposite me. She wasn't alone, she was with the strangest looking man. Considerably older than her, I guessed he was in his sixties. He was wearing a brown raincoat which he kept buttoned up to the collar, and a trilby hat, rather battered yet oddly sporting a bright red and blue feather stuck in the band. He obviously hadn't shaved for days and looked rather down and out. I took an instant dislike to him especially when he spoke. "Good day, young man," he said. A smirk passed quickly across his lips. "A fine travelling companion, I'm sure."

"Hello," I said, more coolly than intended. Blushing, I tried glancing at the girl. The man's eyes held mine, however. Keeping up a continuous stare, he seemed to entrance me somehow. I kept struggling to look away, but my eyes were strongly drawn to his. They were the deepest green eyes and I felt myself sinking into a pleasant, warm reverie. I also felt annoyed – annoyed at him for staring so, annoyed at him for being with her, but mostly annoyed because his staring made me feel so uncomfortable, I couldn't look directly at the girl.

How I wanted to look closer at her features and see if she was really the girl from my childhood encounter. She certainly looked the same, several years older, of course, but arousing in me the same yearning. She nestled up to the old man and seemed so intimate with him that waves of jealousy and disgust welled up from my belly and stuck in my throat. I think I may have even choked a little. Then I couldn't stop coughing as I tried to clear my throat. I felt foolish. Even when he released his hold on my eyes, his hold on my emotional state became stronger than ever. How I hated him!

I had almost forgotten the original encounter, so to have her vividly brought back into my memory and, maybe, even manifested right before me was almost too much to bear. My mind raced: could I speak to her? What if this older man was her lover, as it appeared? No, I reckoned I was misinterpreting it. He must be a relative of some kind, maybe he was an uncle or something. I just couldn't accept he could be her father; she was too appealing and he was too – well, just too knowing. He seemed to look right into the depths of my soul. Now whenever our eyes met, however briefly, I saw a slight grin, a knowing grin, creep around the corners of his mouth. Almost a sneer, really. I imagined he was saying, "she's mine, you can't have her."

I felt hotter and hotter, especially when I realised that she was staring at me. I just knew I had to say something. She had placed three oranges on the seat next to her, laid out in a neat row. They were really large, and the brightest orange. Maybe I could comment on them to break the ice. Maybe I could say something about the weather. Maybe I could simply come out with what I was feeling. I had this numbing fear that somehow, if I spoke, whatever I said would be ridiculed. Finally, my words came out. "Those oranges look amazing."

They kept staring and smiling. The girl nestled closer and closer into his side, but made no response to my words. Feeling incredibly tense now, and more uncomfortable than ever, I tried looking out of the window. It didn't work. I kept noticing her skirt was creeping further up her legs so several inches of her pale thighs were showing. She crossed and uncrossed her legs a few times and I felt myself blushing. I was sure she was doing it on purpose, teasing me. Her legs seemed to hypnotise me as powerfully as the man's gaze had done. I tried looking out of the window at the countryside speeding past – and saw their reflections, their eyes fixed on me. I had never felt so uncomfortable before. I closed my eyes momentarily, but that felt worse, as if the old man's piercing eyes were only inches from my face.

"Tickets please!" The guard startled me as he came into the carriage, but also brought a sense of relief. He looked so normal in his navy-blue uniform with his silver ticket puncher poised ready to make the necessary holes in our tickets. I fumbled in my pockets, unable to find my ticket. I knew it was in my top shirt pocket – I always keep tickets there – but I couldn't find it.

I was blushing again. The old man and the girl both stared and smiled. The guard appeared impatient, but the more I fumbled the more I couldn't find the ticket. "Can I see your ticket please, sir?" said the guard, unnecessarily, baring his teeth with apparent excitement and aggression. I could tell he was sure he'd caught someone without a ticket. I was making his day! By now, acutely embarrassed, I was mumbling a few words and feeling in the same pockets for the third or fourth time.

Standing up, the old man took out his wallet, extracted what looked like a blue business card, and handed it to the guard. Much to my surprise, the guard almost saluted the old man, had one quick and disdainful look at me and left the carriage. My relief was overshadowed by my amazement. Both the old man and the girl laughed as he sat back down. Reaching into a side pocket, he pulled out a battered looking mouth-organ and raised it to his lips. This was becoming surreal. He started to play and how he played! The sounds that came from his mouth-organ were incredible – a kind of bluesy jazz filled the carriage with light. It felt as if all three of us had always been travelling in this carriage, that we were a family of three travelling on some endless and totally joyous journey. I relaxed and laughed a little, suddenly feeling not the slightest bit embarrassed anymore.

The girl picked up the oranges and started juggling them. She was good, too, controlling the fruit perfectly as she stood up. Continuing to juggle, she started doing a crazy little dance around the compartment. I couldn't believe my eyes. I felt so happy. I felt the sense of union with her that I felt at our first meeting in the back lane those several years before. For it was she, I now knew. I recognised her and the more I looked at her face, the more I felt myself sinking again into total communion with her beauty, with her energy, with her easy and joy-filled soul.

The old man's playing speeded up and the girl matched her dance to the music, faster and faster, still juggling as she spun around, her skirt lifting up and revealing her thighs. I admit it: I was completely turned on! I didn't care any more about the old man and his staring eyes. I didn't feel an iota of embarrassment, here I was making love with the girl of my dreams. At least, feeling an orgasmic union with her, yet not having touched her, not even lightly. That was to change, suddenly and strangely, however.

Becoming giddy, or seemingly so, she swirled round and round, dropped two of the oranges and collapsed into my lap. I felt her warm body land on my legs. She wrapped her body into my belly, and I could feel her heart beat, her heavy breathing. I could smell her sweet sweat. We merged, blissfully. I closed my eyes and felt ecstatic ripples of energy coursing through my whole being. It was like a dream come true. If I'd stopped to think about it, I wouldn't have believed it possible. But I didn't stop to think, I simply let go into the gloriously exciting and fulfilling feeling of having this girl, my soul mate, pressed tightly into my lap.

I don't know for how long I had my eyes closed. I felt her breathing slow down and she climbed off my lap. The music had stopped. What on earth had happened? What had we all done? With some trepidation, I opened my eyes, wondering, yearning, yet starting to feel fearful again. Who were they? What had they done to me?

They had gone, I was quite alone. I immediately realised I had been dreaming. That was the only explanation, and I badly needed an explanation. My body still felt released and high, but my mind raced on, thinking wildly, trying to work it all out. Then I noticed a strange sensation in my lap. I looked down and I felt as if my belly rushed up into my throat. It felt as if I hadn't held it back, all my insides would have spewed out of my gaping mouth. Nestled right up into my crotch was the largest, brightest orange I have ever seen.

The Encounter

I couldn't wait to get home. Rushing into my bedroom, I threw off my clothes and lay naked on the bed. Eagerly I peeled and bit into the orange. The juice spurted from the flesh. My fingers dripped the fresh, tingling juice onto my chin, my chest, my belly. My lips parted, saliva almost foaming between my teeth. My male energy straining so hard. And the taste, ah, the taste!

I lay back, ecstatically. Merging with the sound of the clock ticking at my bedside, I felt time stand still. Holding my eyes tightly closed, I felt myself being bathed in light. I lay still, I didn't move, didn't touch myself. I let my body slowly relax. I was still lying there when the light faded and the room darkened.

I had vaguely noticed the wind getting up earlier, but now I realised there was quite a storm blowing up outside. The room was pitch black. As I lay there listening to the wind, I distinctly made out a quite different sound. In the distance, not louder than the wind, and yet strangely present to my ears.

I wouldn't believe what happened next except I know it did. I don't know what it was, but it was as if something alien flew over me from left to right. As it did so. I was enveloped in a radiant buzzing sound. This was so unexpected and truly terrifying that my whole body became rigid. It may have only lasted a few seconds but it felt timeless. I was trapped in a solidity I had never experienced before. I was screaming, but silently for the solid air encompassed everything including my screaming throat. Then it was past. I took a big deep gulp of breath and relaxed, glad this experience was temporary for it had felt far from that whilst it was happening.

Then, at some distance to the right of where I lay, it started again. The throbbing, buzzing sound built up as it became louder and, apparently, nearer. I had no choice but to experience it again but this time I was prepared. Relaxing as deeply as I could, I focussed on keeping my breathing deep and steady. The sound became louder and the vibration stronger, overwhelmingly so. As I relaxed instead of becoming rigid, I felt a deep flow of quivering energy fill my body with the deepest, greatest pleasure imaginable. I couldn't think anything but, if I had been able to do so, I would have known that I was experiencing what Wilhelm Reich, the psychologist, called streaming, the free-flowing energy of orgasm with no physical restriction. The previous experience of rigidity had seemingly lasted for ages although it was truly only a few moments. The ecstatic shaking also lasted for only a few moments but, in it, experiencing it, it never could end because there was no beginning, middle or end to it, it just was. I became the experience itself.

This time it came with words; not in the experience but directly as the sound faded off to the left, as if going back the way it had originally come. I heard words as if spoken by a female voice of great depth and compassion. I didn't get to write it down clearly, but I discovered in the morning that in my bedside dream diary was a hastily written scrawl.

"I love you for who you are, not what you do, and what you do is beautiful, now."
"No more wanting; no more yearning, no more seeking; no more desiring."

My mind was overwhelmed by the experience during the night and, at the time, I paid little attention to the words I had written. I felt elated and yet, at the same time, a strange sense of what I might now call existential angst: what was the purpose, the meaning in my experience? What possible significance could this unbidden experience have for me? I was split: my body felt a new vigour and strength, an easiness, a looseness unlike how I had felt as recently as the night before. At the same time my mind was full of doubt, confusion and disbelief. Had I been visited by aliens? Could this be an encounter with aliens, as it were? Or perhaps it was some kind of breakdown that my brain had interpreted in a dream-like way? Had I somehow made it all up? Had the experience of spontaneous energetic streaming been real – my body certainly felt good, so it seemed so, but ... but ... well, I didn't know what the but was, but there was most definitely one there. I felt determined not to spoil an experience of such profundity and depth with a slick meaningless overlay of fantasy whilst aware it could hardly be anything but fantasy.

As it happened, that morning I had a pre-arranged café meeting with a recently made good female friend called Paula. We had met in a bookstore when I had recommended a book to her with, of course, the intention of getting off with her. From the beginning she was having none of that, she wanted us to be friends. She said we had a special connection, she felt it strongly but that it wasn't sexual. I willingly went along with this but held the hope our friendship might evolve into something more.

Paula was already in the café when I arrived. She looked me up and down, her face awake with surprise and interest. "You've grown!" she exclaimed. Standing back, she exaggerated her look of surprise and laughed. "I'm sure you are taller than last time we met." I argued with her, that this was impossible.

She didn't know me that well, she was mistaken, she was being ridiculous insisting this was true. She was having none of this and, as she asserted so strongly that she was right, there was only one solution, to go back to my flat and measure my height. Rather awkwardly we drank our drinks and ate our cakes. I couldn't understand why, but I felt annoyed with her unwillingness to let go of her ridiculous idea, at least partly – although I wouldn't admit it to her – because standing next to her I did feel taller.

Back at my flat we measured my height; I had been just a smidgeon under six foot tall since my mid-teens and now I measured six foot two inches tall! The effect of the energetic streaming on my body had apparently loosened my viscera, counteracting twenty plus years of gravity, I truly had grown taller. I was shocked. Maybe the whole experience was somehow unreal but that my body had changed was undeniable. Paula stayed with me the rest of that day helping me to try to understand what had happened but we were left with more questions than any kind of answer. And she still wouldn't sleep with me.

The Jumble

Truthfully, I hadn't been to a jumble sale for many years. Something made me decide to go into the big hall beside a church near where I lived, but I did so with no particular interest. It was a large jumble sale: there were stalls round the outside of the hall covered with what seemed to me to be mostly junk. There were big piles of clothes but I had no intention of buying any of these; apart from the fact I felt sure they wouldn't suit me, I just don't actually fancy wearing second-hand clothes. I know it's silly really but I just feel I don't ever want to be wearing something that someone had been wearing when they died.

At the far end of the hall there was one stall entirely covered with scarves. It was very colourful which is what initially drew my attention. It was then I saw her, rummaging through the scarves. I was immediately reminded of when I saw the poor girl going through the dustbin. Coincidentally, at that moment, she glanced up and our eyes briefly met. I looked away, quickly realising this was no fancy from my past but a young girl of maybe twelve or so – as the girl had been all those years before. Embarrassed, I mooched about, realising how foolish, even dangerous it could have been to just look at such a young girl.

An area at the centre of the hall had the large items for sale which included old furniture: a table or two, some stools and chairs, and a fancy looking sideboard with ingrained marquetry. Then I saw her again, sitting on an old sofa in the midst of this jumble. This time I couldn't help noticing her well-developed breasts which were only barely concealed in a cotton blouse. I realised she was not a child at all but older, probably in her early to mid-twenties. Trying to look cool, I walked over and sat next to her.

"Hi," I said. "This is pretty tiring, it's all so busy and rushy."

She smiled widely. "Yes, but I've got some good bargains. What have you got?" I smiled and held up my two empty hands. Pulling items from her shoulder bag, she started to show me what she's acquired. "This scarf, look at the pattern … and this blouse, and this, look!" She held up an extremely thin cotton dress. "I'm not sure I have the nerve to wear this." She laughed.

"I'm sure you could." I was feeling less embarrassed and more embarrassed at the same time. I kept noticing her blouse revealed the shape of her breasts and her nipples pushing upwards through the cotton material. I may have seemed cool on the outside, that was my intention anyway, but I was all a-quiver inside. Here I was talking to – I didn't even know her name – the woman of my teenage fantasies. Or was it her? How could it be? I didn't know, or care really, I just so wanted it to be her. I took the plunge and, holding out my hand, introduced myself,

"I'm Rose," she replied, taking my hand and giving it a serious shake.

I asked her if she went to many jumble sales, if she lived locally, did she work – she ran a shop apparently – and a dozen other questions, but there was really only one question I wanted to ask her As we seemed to be getting along famously, I risked it. "Would you like to come back to my flat?" I asked, adding quickly, "uh, for a coffee and –" I felt very nervous and embarrassed asking, expecting a rejection, but she interrupted me before I finished my clumsy invitation.

"I'd love to," she said and, standing up, continued, "I'm finished here. Shall we go now?"

I couldn't believe my fortune. Here I was, walking down the street, chatting easily to the young woman of my dreams – not any dreams but my deepest, wildest dream since puberty. The dream of finding, befriending and having a relationship with the girl I fell in love with all those years before. "Whoa," I reminded myself, "take it easy, just because she is coming to your place for a drink doesn't mean she is the one."

It was only a few minutes' walk to my flat. I was nervous but she seemed truly impressed. It was a great flat, being the attic floor of an old town house with amazing views over the city rooftops. I made some tea – she, like me, preferred tea to coffee – and we sat in my armchairs and looked at one another, maintaining long, languid gazes. She looked just as I had always imagined – wished – she would look with her shoulder length, dark brown hair, her pretty round face with almost too large eyes and delicious lips I wanted to kiss.

"Shall we kiss?" she asked. I was taken aback; it was so forward. She had read me correctly though and, of course, I responded positively. It was a tenuous kiss, more a peck really, and we both let out a big sigh as we released our anxiously held breath. We laughed together and that really broke the ice. We hugged closely and had one long, luxurious kiss. I held back from using my tongue but, within a second or two, her tongue was in my mouth. Our tongues intertwined and it became a full blown, erotic kiss. I felt my juices rising. We broke for more breath, smiling, looking deeply into each other's eyes.

"I've got to go," she said.

I looked quizzically at her as I felt a rush of disappointment, wanting to say, "You're so beautiful, I love you." Deeper beneath that, something inside me was saying, "I want you. I need you …" but instead I clumsily asked her: "Do you want more tea?"

"No. I'd better be going now."

"Are you sure?" The words that came out of my mouth no way matched my inner feelings of despair and disappointment. Why couldn't I express what I needed to, what I wanted to say to her? I was already disappointed in myself, judging myself harshly. Somehow I blurted out, "I'd like to see you again."

"Yes," she replied with enthusiasm. I'm not sure my self-judging part heard her that way, though. "I'll come round tomorrow when Tom is holding the shop." She looked at me in a way I didn't really understand but it made me shiver. "If I don't get home soon Tom will be angry and I hate making him angry. He gets so upset with me …" Her voice tailed off.

So she had a boyfriend. I was crestfallen. It must have

shown – she moved close again and gave me such a tight hug. "I would choose to be with you right now," she said, "but I have to be honest and real. I'll get it sorted, don't worry." There was another long pause. She broke the hug and said clearly, "I will be back tomorrow," turned and left.

Next day I waited in all day, constantly looking out of the window hoping to see her coming up the road, but she didn't show. I felt so miserable, let down, angry, disappointed, fearful, with a lot of self-judgments about not being good enough. On the other hand, maybe her boyfriend was holding her prisoner or threatening her and she needed rescuing? I realised that was the old fantasy and that I had grown out of the idea of being her rescuing knight. No, it must be me at fault. Maybe she didn't like my kissing. Maybe she thought I was too old for her, or too straight, or not handsome enough. Not tall enough, or too tall – she was quite short – I just didn't know. All these, and more worse fantasies about myself, kept going through my head. How could I have ever imagined such a stunningly beautiful woman would want to be with me? She probably came to my flat out of curiosity and was keen to leave as soon as possible. But the kiss felt real. What was I to do?

As it happened it was easy to deduce the address of the shop she ran because she'd told me it was a unisex boutique at the top of Steady Hill, a well-known spot in town, and there was only one such shop there. I decided to send her a brief letter. 'Dear Rose,' I wrote, 'I so enjoyed our meeting. I would be pleased to see you again if possible. Please get back in touch.' I added my phone number and, after much deliberation of how to sign it, wrote 'with love from' – daring, but it felt honest. I posted the letter and waited. Days, then week or two went by and there was no reply. I guessed that was the end of that. I had found her and yet somehow lost her again.

About one month later, I was walking down a street in town and I saw her approaching in the other direction. My heart started to beat strongly and heavily, nervously fluttering, I felt so on edge. She saw me, smiled widely and almost ran to hug me.

"I'm so sorry," she said, "I haven't dared to get in touch though I've really wanted to." I asked if she had received my letter. "Oh yes," she replied, "and I have kept it precious. I have a hiding place in my bedroom wardrobe and your letter is there. It's treasured."

"Then why, oh why haven't you contacted me?"

"It's Tom, my boyfriend," she replied. "He is rather edgy and previously he has threatened to kill himself if I left him for someone else. Thing is, I think he means it. He's a nice guy but I don't love him, but what can I do?"

"Come and be with me."

"No, I can't, not now – but I am working on it…" She tailed off with an apparent note of sadness. "I'm a captive, really," she said. "Tom is so sensitive and gentle I can't do anything to harm him."

"But then you are his prisoner!" I exclaimed.

"No, not really, it is my heart that holds me prisoner," she replied softly. "But my time is almost done. Then, then I'll be with you. Will you wait?"

I told her I would but that she must keep in touch, to let me know how it is going. I could respect her care for her boyfriend but he was blackmailing her and it wasn't nice. She cried a little. Then she was gone.

A month or more went by and I knew once again I was not going to see her. I was very depressed but it all seemed something of a dream, the jumble sale and the kiss and everything … I knew

I had to let go. Should I contact her again? I decided not, I would only inflict more pain on myself. I was shortly leaving to go and live in London so I decided to just let her go. I had to move on, I felt it was the only way, but inwardly I was depressed. Very depressed.

The Boyfriend

A few months after my meeting with Rose I was back in my old town for the weekend to visit Stan, a long-standing friend. He told me that he had recently taken psilocybin mushrooms and had a wonderful spiritual experience. He wanted to share the experience with me. With trepidation I agreed. The next morning, Stan made some tea using about fifty of these mushrooms, stewed it for a while and then we drank a cup each. I was very nervous, but after a while the effects started and I felt joyous and filled with bright energy. Stan suggested we go for a walk. He knew the town better than me and he led me round street after street I had never even noticed before, telling me bits of history as we went – all this whilst the psychotropic experience revealed streets, people, the ground, the sky – everything – in a new, engaging bright light. Fantastic.

I had no idea where we were when, turning a corner, I found myself standing outside Rose's shop. I had previously told Stan about Rose and he had purposely brought me here, going by a circuitous route to make sure he got me to this place. He knew I wouldn't have agreed if he had told me his plan.

"What are you doing?" I almost shrieked at him.

"Go on," he said, "go inside, go tell her how you feel. Take her, she wants you, you want her, make it real!"

I felt I had to meet the challenge. I would have probably

felt that anyway but the effect of the psychotropic mushrooms was to make it impossible to not do so. I peered into the shop window where several dresses were hanging, all bright colours against a very dark background. You couldn't see into the shop itself, or so I thought, then as my eyes accustomed to the different light, I realised that I could see inside after all. There, looking straight back out at me, was Rose, smiling.

I went in, my heart in my throat, my belly full of jitters. It was so dark in the shop I could hardly make anything out. I could see a man, presumably her boyfriend, hanging about near the back and there, right in front of me, was Rose. I felt tongue-tied and all I could think to say was hello. An incomparably long silence followed; maybe only because of the psilocybin, but it seemed interminable. It was up to me to say something more and I didn't know what. Finally, with great difficulty, I blurted out, "I want you." Gosh, what would she say to that?

"Come see me Monday morning," she said with a smile whilst, seemingly to me, glancing quickly over to her boyfriend somewhere behind. It was the best response I could have hoped for. I understood it to mean she wanted me, too. My heart felt instantly filled with joy.

"I will," I replied and rushed out and charged off down the road. The rest of the trip was magnificent. I felt on top of the world, as if everything in my life was now fitting into place. Stan had wonderfully tricked me into taking a risk and now Rose was inviting me to go to see her. We would be together; I knew it now. What more could I want from life?

Monday morning soon came. I hadn't slept much I was so excited, so nervous, so energised. I bathed, dressed in some of my best clothes and set off to the shop where Rose was awaiting me. I wondered what the boyfriend would think of this: would he be there? Would he be aggressive? What might happen? No matter, I was now set on a course that couldn't be stopped. My will to be with Rose could not be thwarted.

I entered the shop and there he was. I wasn't having any truck with him so immediately said, "I'm here to see Rose."

"No prob," he replied somewhat laconically. "Go up to the top floor, the door on the right."

I was surprised he was so cool about it but I didn't care what he felt. I was nervous, yes, but my excitement was at such a high pitch. Arriving at the door, I tapped lightly. I heard her voice immediately. "Come in," she called.

I entered a rather scruffy bedroom, lit by the morning sun blazing through the window and across a double mattress on the floor. There was Rose, sitting up in bed, smiling widely at me. And, next to her, a man! What? I was so confused.

She clambered out of the bed, looking adorable in baggy pink pyjamas with little animals, I think they were elephants, all over in a darker pink. I wasn't looking at her pyjamas, though, but at her face. She appeared radiantly happy to see me and hugged me briefly before returning to the bed. "This is Tom," she said, indicating the man in the bed, also now sitting up. He greeted me warmly and said Rose had told him I was coming.

I couldn't understand, this wasn't what I had expected or wanted. Nothing like it. The man downstairs in the shop wasn't her boyfriend at all! And here she was introducing me to her boyfriend as if – well, as if there was nothing else between us. What could I do? I could either leave straight away or … so I sat down on the edge of the mattress bed. "I thought perhaps we would be" – I censored what I said – "uh, friends."

"Of course," she said, "I want to be friends with you. We can all have fun." So saying, she seemed to include Tom. We chatted in a gentle, friendly manner some more. I can't remember the content at all, I felt more out of body than I had been with the psilocybin. After some while, maybe half an hour, I left.

I felt like a wounded animal, my tail between my legs. Yes, I could be friends with her and her boyfriend – actually he seemed rather nice – but that wasn't what I had wanted, I felt deserted. I was so miserable for days. I shared all this with Stan, he was very helpful – many more fish in the sea and all that – but I knew I had lost my other half, the woman I was meant to be with. The only consolation was thinking how we had met so serendipitously and maybe we would meet again. Well, that didn't happen until about two years later.

I was living in London still but was back visiting some friends. Saturday afternoon we were walking down a main shopping street, a group of young males together. We were larking about, generally being 'male' and having fun. One of the guys was always commenting on and scoring women out of ten as they passed. "Here comes a twenty out of ten!" he exclaimed.

You've guessed, it was Rose. She greeted me warmly and we hugged. My friends almost fell over with surprise. As Rose and I clenched together tightly she whispered in my ear. I remember the words as if yesterday. "I will always be with you," she said. I didn't understand and went to pull away, perhaps in some way she was mocking me. Meeting her now reminded me of how upset I'd been, how let down I felt by what had seemed to me to be a cruel betrayal.

"But you are my man," she continued, softly for only me to hear. "We may not be together physically but I always hold you in my heart. I feel like you are my other half. I love you." She was managing to shock me yet again but before I could respond she moved back and then she was gone.

My friends were full of it. They wanted to know how I knew her. One even seriously asked if she was a film star. They all thought she was the most beautiful women they had ever seen, but I wasn't hearing any of this. I was feeling a surging sense of understanding something new. Of course, I connected deeply with how she felt. I was her other half just as I felt she was my other half. I didn't have the language to express it this way then, but she was my anima, my inner female, just as I was her animus, her inner male. Not that I understood what this meant. It all was falling into place on a deep feeling level if not yet cognitively.

This realisation didn't make not having her in the flesh any better. I yearned for her body for a while. More importantly, I knew that whoever I entered into a deep relationship with could be truly themselves and not just a projection of my anima. My inner relationship with my inner other, my anima, is my deepest soul connection. I felt such gratitude to Rose, love so deep it transcended any of the physical disappointment. Well, so I tell myself now, but I truly suffered before I could even vaguely reach such an understanding.

The Many and the One

Even though I got it, I didn't; old habits die hard. I tried my best to find the actual, physical woman who would be my anima, my other half. I knew she couldn't manifest as Rose but I somehow expected her to appear in another guise, in another form that I would somehow recognise. Of course, I was older, and maybe a little wiser, so I didn't expect it to happen in an instant. I gave all my 'candidates' enough time for me to find out if they were 'it' or not. I was trying to find my other half in a search that remained primarily outwardly directed.

I learned that the term anima is sometimes used to mean the soul or inner self of an individual as opposed to the 'persona', or outer aspect of the personality. For me, this Jungian interpretation made much more sense at that time. Jung described the animus as the unconscious masculine side of a woman, and the anima as the unconscious feminine side of a man. The anima is the totality of the unconscious feminine qualities a man possesses, and the animus the masculine qualities within a woman. Jung believed that the anima and animus manifest in dreams and influence a person's attitudes and interactions with the opposite sex. To find your anima, if you are a man, or animus if a female, is a major step in the individuation process which cannot happen fully without awareness and connection.

After many years of searching, I let go of expecting to find anima manifest in another person having realised what I was looking for was inside not outside. Indeed, as the interests and engagements of life and career took hold, I pretty much left all this behind. I knew all I wanted to know about animus and anima. It was a great idea that I explored in various ways. I felt quite strongly in touch with my inner female side and, apparently, most people seemed to find me sensitive and empathic. But ultimately life goes on and other matters drew my attention.

I was lucky to meet a wonderful woman with whom I wanted to spend my life irrespective of all this stuff about the other half. I just let that go. In fact, she was a strong woman who exactly fitted the bill as being my anima manifest, in touch with all sides of herself. But I hadn't chosen her, nor, for that matter, her me, for these reasons. It was more simply we fell in love, whatever that means, and just knew we wanted to be together. We fantasised that we had met many times before in previous lives: we'd been family, mother, father and child to one another at various times and our being together was just meant to be.

This strange but compelling sense of past life connection rekindled my interest in esoteric literature. I came across the Rosicrucians, an initiatory movement that claimed to know secrets and truths from the ancient past, especially concerning the role of humankind and of each man and woman on the earth. Their main symbol is the image of the Rosy Cross, a rose flowering at the heart of a cross. It is said to signify the suffering we have to go through in life in order to fully open the heart. Opening the heart is symbolically equivalent to the blossoming of the rose on the cross.

One sunny Sunday afternoon I was looking at the colourful image of a Rosy Cross that I had painted whilst reading a text on the subject and contemplating a deeper meaning in the symbol. This was especially so as it reminded me of Rose, my 'anima figure' from so many years previously. The Rosy Cross is sometimes alternately called the Rose Cross and I think that it was simply this which brought her into my mind. I recalled many of the incidents described here, some of them so fantastic. Mostly, I felt the strongest energy remained from that fateful day when I opened the gate to the back lane and saw her for the very first time.

The new realisation was, for me at that precise moment, stunning. The cross is male and the rose is female so the Rose Cross represents the synthesis of the animus and anima, the moment of becoming fully Oneself. The human experience of falling in love is an externalized moment of this enlightenment; a presage of the union between our temporal nature and our eternal nature. The Rose Cross is the Holy Grail, the Philosopher's Stone, the ultimate aim of the inner alchemy that is achieved through a true loving relationship. Subject and object are united in a Mystic

Marriage, finding Oneself through loss of self in another.

I was so full of this understanding I wanted more than anything to share it with my partner. I rushed from my study into the very long, narrow kitchen in our house. From where I entered, I could see the back door at the far end of the kitchen and my partner at the end of the garden, looking very distant. At that moment she turned and started walking towards me. I waited, leaning against a kitchen cabinet, slightly breathless as she approached me slowly and steadily across the garden and then through the back door. Very slowly, she came closer and closer. I saw she was carrying a beautiful red rose, which, reaching out, she placed on my heart.

"I love you for who you are, not what you do, and what you do is beautiful, now," she said, emphasising the last word with firm kindness. I nodded my assent. I knew these words so well from my experience all those years ago when I had received the 'communication' from my unconscious.

Stepping towards me, she turned her back to me. She said something softly then, but I didn't catch the words. Closing my eyes, I waited, my breathing easy and calm, if a little fast. There was no fear left, no attachment to my soon to be lost old identity, nor excitement really. Just a vibrancy, an acceptance.

She took another step backwards and her body space coincided with mine. Two beings, separate and yet occupying the same space.

"We are one, we are none," I said softly as I felt her silently disappear.

My heart fluttered. Opening my eyes, I saw the world for the very first time.

♣

Nothing Like a Hole in the Head

I first met Clive in a pub which was unusual in itself because I don't usually go to pubs. It was one of those chance encounters one wonders about afterwards; was it was meant to be on some deep cosmic level or would I have been better off not going into that pub that day. I remember it was a hot summer's day. I was on a long walk along a canal and the pub garden looked most inviting for a cooling drink. Duly purchased, I sat at a table in the garden and, nodding, greeted the only other customer there. A guy of about forty, the most striking thing about him was his clothing: a bright blue baseball cap plus a bright red shirt and pair of trousers in an extremely clashing green. I didn't mind when he asked if he could join me, despite his somewhat eccentric appearance.

"Hello," he said, somewhat formally, "my name is Clive and I've got something you want too."

I doubted that and immediately felt alarmed that I had invited some kind of weirdo to join me. It was to be a brief encounter though, and, as there was nothing else to entertain me as I quaffed my drink, I asked him what was this something I would want.

"A hole in the head," he replied.

I didn't mean to be rude but I laughed out loud. It was a surprising answer and confirmed I was wise to be on my way sooner rather than later. "I doubt I'd want that," I said and tried to disengage from the conversation.

"Let me show you." Leaning forward, he slightly uncovered the front of his head by lifting up the baseball cap he was wearing. Clive's bald and seriously freckled forehead shone brightly in the early afternoon sun and I could see, just at the top of his forehead, a small plaster over what looked like a lump on his flesh. On either side, equidistant from the central plaster, were two small scars or dents. The skin around the two small dents somehow brightly reflected the sunlight, but the central plaster revealed nothing. "I can't see a hole," I said.

"Well, the skin heals over, but it leaves a visible depression on my forehead. But I can't show you the hole just now, it's under cover." I winced slightly; this was getting weirder. "I'd better tell you how I got the hole in my head."

There was no harm in humouring him, I thought, and the situation was somewhat intriguing so I took a deep sip of my drink and indicated that I was ready to hear his story. I expected it to be interesting in a ridiculous sort of way.

"It all started many years ago, 1971 to be exact, when I bought a copy of an alternative hippie mag called Gandalf's Garden. I wasn't a hippie type and had never taken any drugs at all – I only ever drank an occasional beer – but the magazine's multicoloured cover attracted my attention. On a whim I bought it. Issue 5 it was, I remember it well. It changed my life all because there was an article titled 'I need enlightenment like I need a hole in the head'. I've never forgotten this title, either. I'd not come across anything like it before. I was fascinated. The article described trepanning, this ancient cultural procedure where you had a hole made in your head. It was used to heal all sorts of problems, or at least people believed it would heal them.

"Trepanning comes from the Greek 'trypanon', meaning something that bores into you. Trepanation is the oldest surgical practice and is still regularly done by some African tribes."

"Gosh!" I exclaimed. "Don't tell me you did it yourself?"

Clive ignored my question and continued his obviously well-used and practiced story. "Trepanned skulls are frequently found by archaeologists, sometimes with lots of holes and big ones at that. It is believed by experts that it was successful and the people who had it done survived. We don't know really why they did it, maybe it was religious or spiritual, but at least it may have been to relieve pressure on the brain to make you feel better, or to cure headaches, or even relieve epileptic fits. It still takes place medically sometimes but they don't understand nowadays – they replace the bone whereas it is vital to leave it open to get the full effect."

"What? But wouldn't infection get in?"

"Not if one properly does it."

"Was yours done properly then?" I asked, becoming more incredulous by the moment.

"'Yes and no. I tried back then to get someone to do it, I even prepared all the equipment to do it myself. I bought some anaesthetic gel, a scalpel, four drill bits and an electric drill. I also managed through dubious means to get some syringes and some anaesthetic stuff. Yes, but I chickened out."

"So you were telling me how you got your hole," I said, 'hole' with a strong emphasis, "and now you say you chickened out. So?"

"It all happened quickly at first. I'd pretty much forgotten about trepanning. No, that's not true, I constantly obsessed about it really, but there was no way I was going to do it, I was far too much of a coward and frightened of getting infected, or damaging my brain, or …" His voice tailed off and for a while he looked pensively into the distance. "Two years later I was working in a garden and fell onto the spikes of a rake that had been left lying on the grass.

Three prongs pierced me, the two outer ones these marks, look" – he leaned forward to show me the dents on either side – "but the middle spike just went right in, luckily for me, I guess, not piercing the membrane round the brain. The blood though, gosh I felt like I should be swooning but as the blood flowed I used my tee-shirt to try and stop it dripping everywhere. You know, even right in the middle of the shock of it happening, I thought of the phrase to 'put a sock in it' but I wasn't going to do that, especially as I felt better. Not elated, or happier or anything, just better."

"Phew. Did you go to a doctor?"

"Oh no, it wasn't like that. As I said I felt better."

"But…" I was speechless.

"It felt really quite blissful at first then it slowly wore off and I was only getting occasional flashes of the original effect, so I decided to make the hole a little bigger. I did a lot of research but ultimately it was down to me. I'm not saying it wasn't painful but I just kept picking at the edges of the hole. In truth it never seemed to really get bigger but each time I tried I thought I might just be making the hole a little bigger and each time I got more effects."

True or not, he now had me hooked with his tale. "What exactly are the effects?"

"Truly, each time I improved the hole in those early days, I would immediately feel an effect, initially a drowsiness and a sense I might fall over any moment, like I might go unconscious, then suddenly my vision was filled with flashing colours – red green and blue like I now wear every day – oh, but the colours initially are so magnificent."

"How on earth could you do this to yourself continuously?"

"It wasn't continuous, only a few times, when the effects

wore off. Not the colours and stuff, that goes really quickly, it's what I was left with. What I know you'd want if you really understand."

"I doubt that, but tell me more. Has it ever caused you problems?"

"Not the hole, mate, but it does cause problems between me and other people, especially medical people. I saw a counsellor once, she was really freaked out, I think she thought I was a psychiatric case. She was the crazy one."

"So, what are the negative effects?"

"Tinnitus. It is horrible. But at the same time there is this feeling of relaxation and silence, oh such a deep inner peace. Have you read any Castaneda books?" I told him that I had done so. "Well, it's like what he describes when with the shaman. It turns off the voices in your head, the inner dialogue is turned down and you can hear the sound of the spheres."

"You mean the tinnitus?"

"No, that is it, but not tuned in fully. With the hole I relax, stop my thinking and then I hear it." He paused again for a while, waiting for me to take in what he was saying. "And it brings me great gifts and dreams like you couldn't imagine."

"Try me!"

"Ok, but I need another drink first."

My glass was also empty so I popped indoors and refreshed our drinks and came back, now eager to hear about his so-called impossible to imagine dream.

"Well, the dream started with sounds and the lights so awesome I could hardly believe it was real, for so it felt, then out of the colours he emerged. He came with eleven heads and a thousand arms, each with an eye in the palm, eyes to look for and palms to give compassion. He came for what was left of me. All my partial emotions and covetous thoughts were banished. All my attachments were released and I was received."

He stopped and looked deeply, vacantly into the distance again. I really didn't want to interrupt his flow so said nothing. After what seemed ages, he continued. "I felt nobly born, like I'd been on a path forever and had reached a goal. I entered the red light, like a primal fire. I sat upon a peacock throne with a lotus in my left hand. A deep resonant voice said to me: 'Enter the endless, boundless light beyond the abyss, the life eternal you embody'…"

I guessed this was it, no doubt an amazing dream. I was going to say something but before I could, he continued. "Then the voice showed me, told me to enter the realm of the rainbow buddha. A halo of rainbow light enveloped me and I woke up and the light was still there. It is always there now. I rarely take the cork out since then, except for top up."

We both sat in silence for a while then he spoke again. "There's this club with, I hear, hundreds of people who've done it. But clubs aren't for me and, quite honestly, I'd not want to meet someone with a hole in their head, would you?"

I laughed. "That's just what I am doing!"

"Yes, but I'm ok, some of them are probably quite mad."

"Are they? Mad I mean."

"No, no. There is a proper medical argument for it you know. It changes the volume of blood in the brain and that gives you more energy, able to focus more, to learn and enact your intent. Of course, I couldn't prove it and I don't know what I'd be like if I hadn't had it done, but you know I'm very bright for a sixty-six-year-old."

"Sixty-six!" I exclaimed. "I do not believe you." I had thought him about forty at most.

"Well, it's another benefit. I've got the energy I had as a child and all the inner connections. I'm talking to you because I've read your aura and know you're ok."

This was now getting crazier. A hole in the head was ridiculous but now Clive was talking about reading auras, and, as far as I could tell, lying about his age.

"I know you think I'm crazy. That's ok, people always do, but I think you're the crazy one for not having it done. Not because I say so, either. Hey, you know my testosterone is much higher than it should be for someone my age. No problem being horny is there, ha-ha!"

He chuckled a strange laugh but it was endearing and I laughed with him. I was getting used to Clive's strange demeanour and, well, assuming it really was true, despite his hole in the head.

"You know a baby has a fontanel?" he asked but continued before I could answer. "They call it a soft spot in the skull but really it's their natural hole. Trepanning just brings you back to this natural state. Babies are so lovely, aren't they? Yeah, as we grow the skull hardens, the brain can't expand anymore and slowly over time, as you age, the blood volume decreases. Making a hole in the cranium just allows the volume of blood to the brain to increase then it pulses in its natural way and you know, it gives you a beautiful smile. Have you noticed?"

Clive was bugging me now, I was getting tired of his proselytising, I needed that like – ha ha – I needed a hole in my head! And now, well it was too much. "So, you think of yourself as some kind of improved, perfected being then?"

"No, not at all, I'm still the same old Clive with my personality disorders, hang ups, all the character issues that I've always had. You heard of Robert Bly? He said our shadow is like a big bag you carry round with you, dragging you back from your full potential all the time. Being trepanned simply lessens the amount of stuff you drag around in that bag. Life becomes, well, just easier, nicer."

"Okay, so it sounds great, you could tempt me, but there's no way I'd ever have it done."

"Oh no, I'm not recommending it for anyone. The trouble is, you get above yourself and you talk to people and you tell them how good it is. You're not trying to persuade them, just give them the info they need and then always they react like you have: interested, but no thanks. Well, I don't blame you because if I took my cork out, I'd be pissed off with you now wasting my time, then it would be hard to contain me."

I felt his aggression inside me, as if it was arising in me. I think it must have been some sort of introjection, but at the time it confused me, especially when he continued: "Yes, you know what I feel," he said in a tone as if he was correcting a child, "and you wouldn't want me to know it, would you, but I know everything. I'll take my cork out and you'll see."

"What do you mean? What will I see?" I was feeling spooked, Clive felt dangerous now and I felt like I needed to escape.

"Just sit there!" he commanded sharply. "I'll show you."

So saying, he started to peel back the large plaster that covered his hole. "Someone once said I should put a sock in it but I wasn't going to do that was I, but I got their point. Look!" he exclaimed as the plaster came right off. "So – ta ra!"

I'd noticed the slight bulge under the plaster but now I knew what created the bulge. True to his word, I could see the end of a small cork apparently blocking his hole.

"Do you see it?"

"Yes, I see the cork," I responded.

"Not the cork, you idiot!' he exclaimed. "My emotions set free of course. Here, I'll take the cork right out to show you now." He rose from his seat and moved towards me whilst reaching upwards to his forehead to remove the cork.

I was already rising from my seat, ready to leave. I was breaking out in a sweat and knew I just had to get away. Somehow, when he removed the plaster and I saw the corked hole, it was already too much. I certainly didn't want him to remove the cork and I most definitely did not want to experience his anger again, nor any other of his emotions. Indeed, I now felt so strangely disturbed I just had to leave before, well, before he persuaded me that there really is nothing like a hole in the head.

The Return of Nikodemos

I never thought I'd own a Tesla car, especially not top of the range – and free! No, I didn't win it, and I tried to give it back. Really. It all started when I was reminiscing about people from my past and, as often was the case, my junior school nemesis came to mind. Nik and I both attended a small, private prep school, in the same class, which meant the bullying I experienced was consistent and ongoing for every year from age five to eleven. Truthfully, pretty much every day. Of course, I learned to accommodate it in a way, but it was such a drag – both the bullying and the fact I couldn't share it with anyone. It just wasn't the 'done thing'. It would have been snitching and, apart from it being a socially unacceptable practice. I knew that, if I did snitch on Nik, it would only make matters worse. As it was, most days we played together, had some exciting adventures, even if they usually frightened me. Thinking back all those years ago, I wasn't even sure that Nik knew he was a bully. Maybe his behaviour was a part of his original family heritage; he was always keen on telling me his surname 'Andino' was that of an ancient Greek warrior and meant a strong male like him.

I had previously looked him up on the internet, including in the late Nineties when Friends Reunited was new, and never found anyone with his name. I found several people from my distant past but nothing of Nik. Not that I minded, it wasn't like I ever want to have contact with the bully. It was just curiosity – you know, the stuff that killed the cat. It was just such curiosity which made me look recently. Google is much more effective these days but all I had to search with was his name, Nik, and what I remembered his surname to be, Andino. I knew that might be wrong and, just as before, nothing really came up. There was a Spanish person on FaceBook with the same name, probably others, but none of them were my Nik. Ha! My Nick, what a laugh; if anything I was always his. He was the one in charge not me.

There was a business called 'The Andino Import Company' in the results. I idly clicked it and found the CEO was someone called Nikodem Andino. Searching their site, I soon discovered their CEO was Nik the bully, now, like me, a guy in his fifties. There wasn't a picture, but it mentioned he had been brought up in Wales and attended a prep school so I just knew it must be him. I felt relieved, strangely happy that he was okay, had what looked like a thriving business, and clearly was successful in life. Gosh, this felt like a strange reaction to the bully but it was so long ago I felt no particular current animosity to him. Indeed, I probably felt morally superior in some way for sending him good vibes. And that was the end of it, or so I thought.

It was only a few days later when, going downstairs one morning, I saw an envelope on the front door mat. It was far too early for the postman so, picking it up, curious what it might contain, I opened it somewhat apprehensively and found inside a very fancy looking, shiny black key fob with the word Tesla, a small booklet with Model S written on it and a card that simply said, 'Sorry, Nik'. What? I opened the door to check outside and there, at the end of my drive, was a bright and shiny blue car, a Tesla Model S no less.

This just didn't make sense. How could Nik know where I lived? How come he could contact me just when I had only recently located him? And, for goodness' sake, he was giving me a very expensive car with an apology! For what? For bullying me forty or so years previously? I couldn't believe this was happening. Whatever else it meant, and however it had happened, and however much I loved and desired the car, there was no way I could accept it. I knew I had to contact him, thank him and ask him to take the car away. I didn't want to make any contact but hey, the guy had made this grand gesture and the least I could do is decently refuse his offer. Apart from anything else, giving me a car didn't fix the past, but the past was the past. I decided to phone the number on his business site and to my surprise it was Nik who answered. Even after all those years I recognised something of his voice.

"Is that Nik Andino?" I asked tremulously.

"Who is this?"

Somehow, I didn't even want to say my name. "The person you just gave a car to."

There was a moment's silence. "Robert?" he said questioningly. I had always been called by my full name back in Junior School days. "Hey, man, thanks for calling me. You're Rob now, is that right? I just wanted to make amends, to say sorry. I remember how badly I treated you. I'm so happy to hear you have the car, I know it's not much but I hope you'll forgive me."

I was nonplussed, and annoyed, and I think this come across in my response. "Nik, you can't do things like this. I appreciate the gesture," I said, not totally convincingly, "but I don't want you to give me a car."

"Why not?"

"Why not? Because I have forgotten you years ago and you are forgiven anyway and that's that."

"But you googled me and came looking at my business," he complained.

"Yes, but I didn't expect to find you – "

"Then why look for me, Roberrr – uh, Rob," he retorted.

"I don't want to have this conversation, just come pick up the car please."

"No!" he exclaimed. "It's yours now, it's registered in your name. Take it."

I shouted down the phone line: "just pick it up" and ended the call. My heart was beating, it was almost as if he had started bullying me again. Bullying me to accept a fancy car from him as atonement. I wasn't having it. No more bullying from Nik. He could come and pick up the car and that was that. It took me a long while to settle down, but I decided to just leave the car where it was until he sent someone to collect it. I certainly wouldn't use it.

What I didn't expect was to answer the door the next morning and to find Nik himself standing there. For a moment I didn't know who he was, then he became like an older version of the Nik I knew all those years before, except he'd never have been wearing back then what looked like a very expensive, tailored suit. I was kind of aware it made him look thinner than he probably was but Nik the boy had been very skinny, too. What really held my attention, though, was his dark piercing stare. Yes, there are deep lines in the skin around them; yes, they have rather over-sized and wrinkly bags underneath, but the eyes were the same as ever. His hair didn't seem to have changed much either; a too long back and sides, finished off with what used to be called 'a jaunty quiff' at the front.

"Aren't you going to invite me in?" he asked, almost too keenly.

Of course, I certainly didn't want to let him indoors, but

I also didn't want to seem churlish, and I guess I still felt a little fear, his presence was so intense.

'Some things don't change,' I thought as I nodded, stepped slightly aside and beckoned him in. I certainly wasn't going to ask him into the living room, though, and directed him towards the kitchen. He made some pleasantries about the house being lovely but I decidedly ignored his comments until we were sitting either side of the kitchen table. I couldn't help noticing the carving knife on the kitchen sink and, for no real reason, couldn't help wishing it wasn't there.

"So why don't you want the car?" he asked outright.

"I don't need it," I replied.

"But it's a wonderful car."

"Yes, yes, it sure is," I replied, "but that's not the point."

"Then what is?"

"What do you think, Nik? You were constantly horrible to me for years, making me do things I didn't want to do and..." He tried to interrupt but I stopped him with a strongly raised hand. "Stop, no listen that's past, it's ok, we were kids. Kids do crap stuff, it's so long ago it really, really doesn't matter now." I strongly emphasised the second 'really'.

For a moment he looked crestfallen but quickly recovered. "What do you want from me then?"

"Nothing."

"How about a better car, maybe a different make?"

"You're not getting it, I want nothing from you now or ever."

"Why?"

"Because you were a bully."

"I know, that's why I want to give you a gift. I realise it doesn't make it okay but it's just a gesture, you know –"

43

It was my turn to interrupt him. "Yes, I get it," I said firmly. "Thank you for the thought but no, it's not right." I sometimes can't help myself saying too much and I wished immediately I'd left it there, but I then said: "Anyway, the car costs like a hundred thousand pounds. You can't be that rich to just give away so much."

"Ah well," he said as he leaned forward in a conspiratorial way, "I have more money than I or my family could ever want and I'd be happy to share some of it with you. I really want to make it up to you. I'm a religious person now and it's my way of making amends before I die."

I laughed. "You! Religious! Pull the other one!"

Now Nik laughed. "I don't think you would want me to pull anything, would you?"

I couldn't help laughing too. "No, you are right there." Then I remembered I was upset he traced me just because I'd looked at his business site and saw a chance to ask him how.

"Well, I have these boys work for me who are very tech-y and they look out for me. There are people who'd like to get me if they could."

I didn't doubt that was true. He said it convincingly enough but it just felt right anyway and, of course, I could have been one of these people in the past.

He read my thoughts. "No, no, Rob, you don't understand. My business is, well, dangerous."

Of course, now I was hooked. "How come?" I asked. "Don't you import Greek produce, olives and the like?"

"Rob, can I trust you? It's not all, what you might say, above board really."

"Drugs?" I asked.

"Oh no, more financially lucrative than that. Things that

come from further east, and money that needs special attention."

"Why are you telling me? I could tell the authorities."

"But you were never a snitch!"

"I might be now."

"No, you won't. I couldn't allow that. Look, now we're friends just take the car and let it be."

"Nope. No car, thank you."

"Would you like the money instead?"

"Stop it, Nik, I'm not having anything from you."

"But I've just given you something very big."

"What's that?" I sneered.

"Information, the most powerful thing there is. You know about my business; you have a hold on me that's very powerful."

I don't know what, but I was about to say, but something suitably strong in response when Nik disarmed me, as it were. "So, Rob," he said breezily as he stood up, "I'll come back tomorrow morning at nine, think over my proposition."

"What proposition?" I replied. "There's no proposition."

He smiled and walked out. Here I was being bullied again by Nik. I could have shouted after him not to go, to come back and take his car with him. I could have grabbed that carving knife on the sink and thrust it into him – well, not really, I hope – but all I did was sit there feeling flabbergasted. Why the heck had I started this by looking him up in the first place?

But then another voice in me rather meekly said, 'Yes, but it is a wonderful car.'

The strangest thing for me, after Nik left, was that I actually felt quite warm towards him, like meeting again a really old friend. It made me reflect over the meaning of friendship. In all the years since junior school, whenever I recalled Nik and how he bullied me, I would never have thought of him as a friend. He was my enemy. Not really my nemesis, though the word sounds good, but the most hateful person to my younger self. How could I now have warm feelings towards this monster? Apart from all the past stuff, I felt – and rightly so – that he was bullying me again by trying to force me to accept a gift I didn't want, then kind of threatening me about what he revealed to me of his criminal business. Yet, despite the past, and despite this current stuff, I couldn't help what I was feeling.

Truth is, of course, in those early days in the prep school Nik and I were sort of friends. We were the only two boys in the small class so we inevitably spent time together, but it was more than that. Friendship is a strange thing: you can be friends with someone and not everything is ok in the relationship. Maybe that's the secret of a good relationship, to be able to take the bad as well as the good aspects. True friendship is inevitably imperfect. But then, in all the intervening years, I had only ever remembered the negative, the 'bad' Nik who had mercilessly bullied me. Had there really been good times as well?

It was hard to connect with that as my mind continued to dwell on the negative memories. For instance, we went to the swimming baths once a week. I hated the water and continually felt frightened. Nik was largely responsible for this; he would find at least one chance every week to push my head right under the water and laugh at me for being scared. But it wasn't him who dragged me through the water by a strap tied around my chest and forced me into the deep end. The teacher who did that was the real bully. I can't pretend it was conscious on Nik's part, but maybe on some level he was trying to man me up.

I was truly terrified of the pigs at Nik's uncle's city farm where we went sometimes to play – but, if Nik hadn't forced me, I would never have experienced the joy of riding on the back of a big old pig. We went sometimes to the car park in front of the old Victorian train station and stole pigeons. Nik had worked out how to do this to a tee: a trail of crumbs, a quick grab and the pigeon was speedily imprisoned beneath his school blazer. We took the pigeons back to his parent's back garden where his father had a big cage with racing pigeons where Nik would deposit the captive feral pigeon. I so didn't want to be part of this, and was so frightened we'd be caught red-handed. I have to admit it was a great adventure, though. I guessed his father just set these pigeons free, they weren't like his trained racing birds, but for all I know they might have eaten them.

But then, one time in the station concourse, Nik pulled piles of leaflets from their slots on the wall and scattered them all over the ground. Then, pointing at me, he shouted 'look what he did' and quickly started running away. The bastard. Of course I ran too, my life felt seriously under threat by such behaviour, and it put paid to any idea of an actual friendship. I can't find anything redeemable about such acts even if they weren't as bad as they seemed to be at the time. I know playing rat-a-tat-ginger, for instance, is relatively harmless, and it did add a whole level of fun in to my life I wouldn't otherwise have had. But, and it's a big but, I hated every moment of it at the time and however I tried reframing the incidents I recalled, it didn't make them ok. He was a bully back then and was still a bully now. What could I do?

I didn't sleep much that night. My mind kept going over memories from the past involving Nik and me, but even worse was the argument that continued with myself over the car. Why shouldn't I accept it? So long as I got all the proper, correct paperwork, the car's logbook, ownership papers, whatever, so it was all above board and clearly a gift and … that was the problem, I really was tempted. But then I couldn't seem to help coming back to the dilemma, finding more reasons to make it ok to accept the car. When all was said and done, I deserved it after all the pain he caused me back then. He could obviously afford it with no problem so I wasn't actually taking anything from him. But then what might I be taking from someone else? For all I knew he might traffic in people, for god's sake, or be involved in some other heinous activities.

What was I taking from myself by accepting the car, even by considering taking it? My dignity, my truth, my values. But then he offered you the money instead and that – stop! I will not sell my soul, full stop. And especially to Nik who is clearly an untrustworthy bully as he always was. No, that was that. Of course, it wasn't, but I did doze some before getting up early and awaiting the arrival of Nik. He might not come at nine o'clock, I might be waiting all day for nothing. I knew that, but I had chores to do, so it wasn't wasted time. My mind was really not focusing on much else, though, except the situation with Nik and how I would deal with it.

Nik arrived at nine sharp. I was looking out of an upstairs window and had been watching for him for some while. I wanted to see what kind of car he drove, and, well, to get a measure of him. It also gave me time to gain my composure before I went to the door. I saw him get out of the back of a limousine style car. There were two men in the front, and, having dropped Nik off, the car drove away. There was nothing sinister about it, really, but seeing him having these guys with him really put me on edge. I went to open the door for my old 'friend' with more anxiety than I intended.

"Hi Rob," Nik said, breezing in. I noticed that he was dressed more casually, smart casual, and wondered if it was because it was now a Saturday, or was he trying to match himself to my style? I was suspicious of him immediately.

I planned to be civil, to recall and mention some of the fun stuff we had done together and not refer to the bullying at all. Assuming that all went well, to then raise the matter of the car. I had a lot of questions about the legality of the car and of him gifting it to me. Of course, I knew there was no way I could possibly have the car, but I would somehow persuade the part of me who so strongly desired it to desist from driving me crazy with complaints about how stupid it was to turn it down.

Anyway, all this was irrelevant as Nik disarmed me immediately. Sitting back in the same kitchen chair as the day before, he plonked a cardboard folder on the table and, smiling widely, said, "Here are all the documents proving the car's yours. Everything." He paused momentarily then, leaning forward, said: "I gave you a car once before, you didn't mind then. Do you remember?"

Recovering from this unexpected opening move, as it were, I declared that yes, I did remember the car. "It was a model car, a Renault I really wanted at the time. It was red."

"Yes." Nik seemed genuinely pleased.

I could have stopped there and kept to my plan but blurted out, "But it was a terrible birthday, my worst ever."

"Gosh! Why?"

I didn't want to to discuss it with him at all, and I knew he'd remember nothing about it, so simply said, "Oh some silly upset or another."

"Was it when you lost your slipper?"

I was stunned. How could he know? He was spot on and,

49

that he remembered, confirmed my fear of the time that everyone thought badly of me because of it. "Yes, of course," I replied rather gruffly.

"But it was an incredible birthday."

"No, it was most certainly not!" I exclaimed and started blurting out to Nik my complaints about the birthday.

It was my eleventh, the last whilst still at the prep school, and the first guests had arrived. Agh! I hated any parties because I was so self-conscious, and terrified of being made to look foolish. Most of all I hated my parties, held religiously on my every birthday. It was like a religion, too, one that commanded total obedience from my mother who genuinely believed that I was looking forward to seeing all my friends and having a great time. Like hell I was. Even Nik was coming. Beth, my 'girlfriend' was there, wearing her best party dress, light blue with little yellow flowers on it. Her yellow socks matched the flowers, as did the ribbon in her hair – well, almost. I liked her a lot, though was too timid to show it, even though I knew she liked me, too. Beth went to the same prep school as me and Nik, whose arrival I dreaded. Some of my other more local friends ruled the street culture where I lived and I had to be my best cool with them around. I knew something could go wrong; it always did. But perhaps this time I'd be lucky – we were at least ten minutes into the party and nothing had happened yet.

When Nik arrived, he gripped my hand for a handshake, as always, too tightly for me to pull it away. I started to go red in the face, struggling to free myself whilst pretending nothing was happening. He wished me happy birthday and put a little box in my other hand. God, did I have to open it? He released my hand as if to say yes, you do. I ripped off the paper, opened the box and found a toy car, the Renault that I really wanted. Nik was smiling at me – strangely, or did I imagine that? What plans had he got for me and this car, I wondered? But never mind, this was bearable, especially with the car, so maybe my birthday wasn't going to be so bad after all. A foolish thought.

We got through the meal well. I felt awkward a lot of the time, especially when I had to blow out the candles, but I was coping with it. Only an hour or so to go at the most, I reckoned. Then it would be a whole year till I had to put up with this again! We were playing games now, always a dodgy time. Still, 'postman's knock' wasn't the worst of games.

My mother sent me outside first, almost pushing me through the door with just the force of her words. I made dutifully for the door, opened it and started through into the hall. I don't know how I did it, but, somehow, I stepped out of one of my slippers. I turned to put my foot back in it, but my mother was too quick for me. Picking up my slipper and stopping me having it, she turned to the other children with the darkest, most awful conspiratorial look. Her dark witch had emerged.

I tried to snatch it from her. The more I squealed and shouted, the more everyone laughed, and the more my mother held the slipper away and pushed me through the door, outside.

I wasn't laughing. I was screaming now. I was crying, I felt totally humiliated, totally shamed. My mother pushed me into the hall and closed the door. There was uproar from inside. The birthday boy had been shamed to his socks. Destroyed. I sank into a heap and sobbed intermittently. My mother was so cruel. I hated her. I hated her!

This was a very serious incident in my early development. It affected me profoundly, in how I related to the world and other people. It came up several times during my therapy. I worked on my anger at my mother, her betrayal of me, my shameful feelings.

'But, Will, it wasn't like that!" exclaimed Nik. "I thought more of you because of it, and loved your mother, she was great."

"What do you mean?" I asked, careless of an answer. What could he know of what happened that day, or anything of my mother?

"All I saw was the kindness in your mother's actions. She said she was only teasing you. She held out her hands and she smiled so radiantly I wanted to run to her arms, never mind you. At first, I felt so envious, my mother was never so open with love like that. The love was overwhelming though and, as I said, I wanted to be embraced by her, too. You held out, though, for several moments. Then you just let go and fell into your mother's arms. We all cheered, everyone was laughing, it was so, well, I don't know what we all felt at the time, but now I'd say it was love; the love between you two. I never experienced anything like that, except with your mother."

"What do you mean, with my mother?"

"You really don't remember at all, do you?"

I was starting to feel irritated, but there was something in this meeting, in the energy of the moment, that made me hold myself back from fighting him anymore, I wanted to hear what he thought he remembered. "No, I don't remember anything else. What?"

"I came over, so glad for you, and I slapped you on the back – sure maybe a bit too hard – but I really meant it as a compliment, and your mother reached out, put her arm around me, and drew me in to the two of you."

I couldn't believe what was happening to me. I knew as he spoke it that it was the truth. I remembered. I started laughing and crying.

Nik continued: "And everyone else all crowded round

and we were like one super, free, amazing being. Cheering, whooping, wow, it was far out."

"Yes, yes …" I could hardly take another word, it was overwhelming. A whole edifice I'd created around this incident, which I thought I'd worked on in therapy. All the time it was not as I remembered, or not so much remembered but had reconstructed to make myself some kind of unloved victim.

"I never bullied you after that. Well, we soon moved on to secondary school, you to the high school, me to the comp, and so I couldn't have bullied you anyway. But I wouldn't have. I loved you, man."

Nik stayed with me the rest of the day, we shared so much of all the times we had spent together. A lot of reframing went on, and I laughed till in stitches several times with sheer fun and joy about, yes, even the times he had bullied me. I had really found the most surprising new friend.

At breakfast the issue of the car come up. "You don't need to give me anything, you never did," I said. "Listen, what you've given me is more than a car, to release all that misunderstood energy."

"Don't start that again," laughed Nik. "Now, where's that folder I brought? It's got all the info."

"You bully!" I exclaimed.

53

Whatever Happened to Saul, Paul, David and Catherine?

S *aul today, day dreaming, vaguely listening to the directions from David but not entirely; feeling listless, dreaming largely of the happy house, home, hear what the crows were saying in the trees outside: not seen but felt. He enjoyed his young body, toned muscle hanging on its strong bony structure, lusty at times, and restless inside now from the negative ionisation of the seashore.*

In the atmosphere around Llantwit lay the weight of late summer sunshine, pressing the air on its inhabitants' heads, pushing them down into deep spaces where they sense the summer storm's imminence. What the storm would bring with its breaking none imagined except Saul. He not only imagined, he knew, for in his feelings were memories of past realities. To make a shaman dream you send them off to sleep, and when they wake, they is not the 'one' who was sent to sleep.

Paul awoke to a sorcerer's dawn, a golden dawn, and laughed to see Saul still asleep, his mouth open, his tongue a pink dry dot in the wet circle of night's slack mouth. Paul yawned. Paul stretched. Paul's bones clicked as all sorcerers' bones do. Click. Click. Click. It awoke Saul – eyes opened in a flash and in the same flash he drew himself to his feet and stood before Paul, tapping his left foot like a rabbit and whistling softly his hunter's hum ...

"Cut!" commanded David. He liked commanding; it was his predilection. Since he was now a famous photographer, when he commanded others obeyed. The fashion models relaxed their

pose amidst the Welsh set, constructed in Wales to look more Welsh than Welsh. The click, click, click of the camera still echoing in their ears, the flash, flash, flash of the electronic lights still bright before their eyes, like the blinding white light of the first flash of lightning over Llantwit.

Saul started counting. One second equals five miles. One second. The storm was more than five miles away. Two seconds. More than ten miles. Three seconds. Further than – he never set off for four. The thunder crashed three seconds after the lightning, echoing around the whitewashed houses of Llantwit. That is (in this space-time tunnel, there are aeons of others) the centre of the storm lay fifteen or so miles away. Add the one at the beginning (one being God) to the five at the end (the completed pentagram of the age): Saul did just that and got six-six-six. And the pentagon was now standing on its head, mimicking the face of Satan the Saviour. This time.

Catherine, in a light summer dress, was on the hill behind Llantwit, within the ancient circle of stones laid there by her genetic ancestors for her to remember, or, as she put it, put the parts back together. The pelting rain that accompanied the outbreak of the storm drenched her body and shrouded her in a mist of negatively-ionised rain dust. The rain dust was of voodoo, glowing brightly around her almost naked body. Her long blonde hair clung to her head and shoulders. Her nipples cold, firm, further, further, and every hair follicle on her body was rising. Catherine, a psychic magnet to the centre of the electric storm, searching her out, reaching her embrace. No longer fifteen miles but closing in, fast but gentle ...

The lightning charge waited: for a moment it stayed with Catherine as it closed upon her. She stretched arms up in the posture of Shu, the great sky-supporting God, her image that of the

55

*infinitely small woman who embraces the infinitely larger earth.
She became a point in space, her body a dry pink dot in the wet
circle of the storm's tight mouth. She embraced the flash above the
stone circle above Llantwit, above the sea, above the bottom of the
ocean – to open herself to the full impact of the electricity. Flash.
Click – right in her left ear and standing before her in an alien
landscape was her Angel, erect and ready. A pregnant pause (paws
of the god Pan) but Catherine knew (her contraceptive was the
moon) no physical child would be born of this union.*

Who are these people? Were they figments of my imagination
in 1976 when I wrote this or were they based, at least for their
character, on people I knew? How would their story have
unfolded, I wonder, because I don't know what I had in mind at
all. I do recognise the people who the characters were based on,
although in totally different situations and living very different
lives than these characters.

Saul and Paul are identical twins but, of course, that isn't
their real names. Nor are they, or would they have been, fashion
models for various reasons, not least that one of them died. Their
father was a vicar in Yorkshire, a kind man who always seemed
somewhat overwhelmed by his job. My parents knew the family
through some connection or another and I had contact with Paul
and Saul. I didn't really play with them, though, as they were
about eight years younger than me. Thing is, whilst that is true,
I always found them a little creepy and would not have wanted
to play with them. I couldn't always tell which one of them was
Paul and which Saul. This was not helped by their mother, Mary,
who had the habit of dressing them in identical clothes a lot of
the time. I think she feared showing favouritism to one or the
other, but unfortunately her decisions often involved going to the

lowest common denominator rather than the highest. So, with their fair, curly hair combed over in exactly the same way, their identical blue eyes, and their perpetual twitchiness, once they were dressed the same it was nigh impossible to distinguish one from the other.

Once they spoke, or even more so if they moved more than twitching, then they were quite different. They became like chalk and cheese, jack sprat and his wife, the weather couple – every opposite pair you can think of. I am not overstating this and I was always blown away, even when they were still quite young, by how different they were considering they were identical twins. Saul, the elder by a few minutes, was an introvert through and through; he was reading before junior school and never seemed without a book, often of a religious nature. Paul, the extravert, was mad about sport and physical challenges and strongly turned away from his father's faith.

When I wrote the beginning of the story, I had them loosely in mind for these characters. They were fifteen at the time, or thereabouts, but I was imagining them older, having left home, moved to London, and used their good looks, and that they were twins, to become top fashion models. They were living the high life in more ways than one and were about to become involved in some tale of magic and mystery involving weird numerology and, somehow or another, the devil.

They had always made fun of their own names, partly to compensate for other kids – and adults – making remarks about them both being named after one person in the Bible, Saul who became Paul. You can imagine the teasing they faced from children and the endlessly repeated jokes amongst adults, from 'have you had your conversion on the road to Damascus then, little men?' – a favourite of their uncle Bill, delivered whilst rolling his eyes and patting both their heads – to detailed discussions about Christian theology that went over their heads.

In the life they actually had, however, tragedy struck and they never reached twenty as a pair. Paul had an accident on a motorcycle when they were nineteen years old and, though he seemed to be recovering, some complications emerged and he died. Of course, the family were bereft, but the curious result was Saul, now for the first time alone in life, became Paul. Not literally, but he became extravert, taking on the characteristics and manners of his dead twin. Then, rather like Saul in the Bible becoming Christian and changing his name to Paul, 'our' Saul 'found religion' and followed his father into the church.

Very clearly then, neither of the twins became fashion models as they did in my fictional tale, but Catherine is another story altogether. Back then, I could easily have imagined her doing what I described in the story. In her early twenties, she had a beautiful, energetic body, was loads of fun, but was psychologically and emotionally very edgy to say the least. It felt dangerous to be around her and, on one occasion, I was quite literally frightened for my life.

We had been friends ever since I tried to play a silly trick on her and it backfired. I was at a music concert and I happened to find a house key on one of the tables. Don't ask me to explain why, but it seemed a laugh to walk to one of the female door attendants and say, in a conspiratorial tone: "I've found the key," as if I was some sort of weird cultist.

For a moment, caught off guard, she looked quite concerned then, unexpectedly, she leaned in close to me and replied: "I've always wanted to find the key."

We both laughed, and I showed her the door key in my

hand which she took with a mumbled promise to hand it in. Then, even more unexpectedly, she asked me if I wanted to come to a party.

I was on for it, she looked beautiful with her long blonde hair and big welcoming smile. "So, what kind of party is it?" I asked.

"Oh, you know, a house party. My friend knows someone who knows someone, it won't be a problem."

"You mean it's a private party?" I asked, feeling now rather uncertain about the whole idea.

"Well, it's not a public one," she scoffed. "If you don't want – "

I interrupted her, I didn't want to miss this intriguing and exciting opportunity with a woman who was becoming even more attractive as we talked. "No, no, of course I'll come with you. Where is it?"

"Just out of town, you can drive me there."

"How do you know I've even got a car?"

"Well, you have haven't you?"

"Yes."

"There you are then, it's settled. I'll see you by this door at 10.45 after the last band finish." With that she quickly walked off with the key.

I wondered if I should meet with her. She seemed a little crazy but then no crazier than I was feeling that eve, so I decided to take the plunge and go to her party, come what may.

We met as arranged and I followed her directions to a large suburban house on a quiet street. At the time I had no idea she would ever drive me anywhere, or that she would be so crazy a driver to make me fear for my life. In retrospect, though, the way she nagged me to go faster, not take so long at street corners, and so on, was fully in character. "We don't want go miss anything," she said more than once, eagerly leaning forward as if to make the car go faster.

Apart from some lit-up rooms and the distant sound of some groovy, gentle jazz music, it would have been hard to guess a party was taking place in the house. At the door, opened by what looked like a stereotypical bouncer from a movie, Catherine had the right credentials and we were allowed into a large hall full of tables festooned with all sorts of edible goodies. The music was louder inside but still background and non-obtrusive. A good-looking waiter wearing rather too few clothes offered us drinks – some kind of cocktail – and it started to dawn on me that it was a sex party. Several plates with different flavour condoms on them put me in no doubt.

"Did you know what sort of party this is?" I asked Catherine.

"No, but let's look!' she exclaimed whilst dragging me into a nearby room. Dark, smelling of patchouli, and with several mattresses covering most of the floor, there were half a dozen or so couples in various stages of undress and foreplay and in one corner, in full view, something I never thought I'd see in my life, even if I'd ever thought of such a practice existing, which I hadn't.

Catherine seemed to want to engage as she whispered to me, "it makes me feel hot looking it at them."

"Yes," I said rather more dubiously, "but I don't really want to be here doing this."

"Don't you?"

"Not really no. What about you?"

"Well, if you want to go that's ok with me. Would you like to go back to my place instead and be private?" she asked, emphasising the word 'private' with a suggestive tone.

I couldn't believe she was agreeing to leave so easily but felt immensely relieved, and back at her place she more than made up for what we might have missed at the party.

I also discovered Catherine was deeply engaged in various spiritual practices involving an exotic mix of Voodoo, Occultism and Buddhism. This made her even more attractive to me.

I wanted to see Catherine again but she was having none of it. "You would become attached to me then I'd have to hurt you," she reflected when I expressed my interest. Truthfully, whilst it would have been an adventure to have an ongoing relationship with her, I wasn't too bothered. I reckoned, in the vernacular of the time, that Catherine would be heavy going. However, about a week later, I received a call from her asking if I wanted to go to a party.

"No, this is a nice party, not many people – and no sex as far as I know." She laughed. "We'll be safe with our secret."

"What secret?" I asked, wondering what she meant.

"Oh you know, that we attended a sex party where a man was having his testicles–"

"Yes, yes," I said, not wanting to be reminded of the surreal scene we had witnessed that night. But I did want to see her again. "And back to your place after?" I ventured to ask.

"Oh sure," she replied, then, giggling, she added, "but no sex – as far as I know." She laughed. "I'll come pick you up at eight."

"You've got a car?" I said, surprised.

"For sure I have, it's really fast."

This is how I came to be in Catherine's car, frightened for my life. I was hamming it up a bit but was clawing at the windscreen of her car and trying to open the door to jump out as Catherine, laughing wildly, came straight out of a side road into a heavy traffic zone with no right or left look, no sense of driving etiquette, just straight out. I felt genuinely scared in the car with her.

"C'mon, you big blanket, let go!" she wailed at me as we swung wildly round another corner and sped off towards the party we were to attend.

I couldn't 'let go' as she put it, I couldn't cope with her craziness. I was straight with her, blunt even. "Just let me out here," I demanded. "I really don't want to go anywhere just now. I'm tense, feel weird and definitely not in party mood."

Catherine could put the brake on a car as violently as she drove it. She took me literally, stopped the car just where we were, not even pulling over, and told me to get out. Actually, she screamed at me to get out, which I happily did. That I reckoned was the last time I'd ever see her, and later she became the template for the character in the story, crazy but also deeply connected in some way to her own spiritual path.

Some years later, I happened to bump into her in a Welsh town I was visiting whilst on holiday. I hardly recognised her at first, she looked the classic mother pushing a pram with a young child walking alongside her. I discovered she had really straightened herself out, got married, moved to Wales and was living a very conventional life. It was good to see her and I think she was pleased to see me too, but, despite assertions of how we should meet up again more properly, we parted without exchanging phone or address details.

In my version of her life, Catherine was in Wales which came true, but instead of following some crazy energy leading to an encounter with lightning, earth energy and an angel, she was living a conventional life. Our fantasies about people and what they might do are rarely accurate and, in her case, way off mark.

What about David, the fourth character in my incomplete story? David, who was he? Who fancied himself as a professional photographer when writing this story? Me of course. Indeed, what character in this or any story written by me of any other writer isn't the writer? Further, aren't we all characters in the bigger story of evolution and the unfolding of life on our planet?

So, whatever did happen to Saul, Paul, David and Catherine?

David and Catherine Revisited

Several months after writing the above, I was sorting through some old, handwritten notes from aeons past and came across what appears to be the next instalment in the story of the characters David and Catherine. After digitizing and other magical electronic tricks, my handwriting was converted to text. So, here is what happened next to David and Catherine.

The mountain was very dark as always, but it was the first time David had ever seen it so distinctly black. It was the effect of the bank of clouds rolling in from the north and obscuring the setting of the sun to the west of the mountain. The clouds were as heavy as the mountain itself and seemed to draw their weight from the subterranean water courses that criss-crossed underground then centred on the stone circle at the mountain's peak. The clouds oozed forward, enveloping all in their shrouding weight. To the right of his vision David could still see the outline of the King Stone silhouetted against the orange and red sky. As his gaze swept slowly to his left, David saw the front edge of the clouds, their soft but ragged, curling edges lined with a brilliant red flashed with silver. He stared long and hard at the edge of the clouds. He imagined Catherine, somewhere amidst the stones, was staring there too.

The more he looked, the more he could make out faces – strong, looking, angry god-like faces with straggly, swirling beards. Staring, David felt drawn to the cloud's movement; always there, always cloud but always changing. He felt his mind snap with the realization that his beliefs and ideas, indeed all his feelings and sensations too, were ever changing. It was not a new realization, he had it many times before, but this time it was like his mind gave up and turned off. He was no longer staring hard but, despite his relaxed gaze, the edge of clouds appeared nearer than ever. The King Stone itself was now enveloped; David knew – without thinking it – that Catherine had been enveloped by the same clouds. He felt a caress, cold to the touch but warm inside, that he sensed was Catherine's feelings rather than his own. Her image appeared before him, distant but growing, as if it rapidly zoomed into his awareness from some remote, unconscious spot in the totality of himself. Then – in a flash – he was reoriented and he realized it was not Catherine who moved but himself. He knew deep inside himself that although separate they could never be really apart because they were One. Exaltation prickled through him.

Now he was lying at a forty-five-degree angle on a slab of hard, cold stone. To his left the cold cloud mass caressed his body with its icy tentacles. To his right the sun gently and lovingly touched his naked body. The wind whistled strange syllable-like sounds in his left ear, the same syllables repeated over and over as if by a thousand voices in a harmony of whispering. The voice of the sun in his right ear was one long 'aaaahh' of gentle but deep delight. He felt his thighs parting, slowly welcoming the sun's insistently teasing touch. 'He' was Catherine, calling to Pan: and 'he' was Pan, astride the cloud, rushing on Catherine with the ice-cold juices of a god and the warming caress of a Goddess. As Pan 'he' was male and female; as the lover of Pan, Katherine and 'he' were neither male nor female, but rather one soul, unsplit, unsexed and at the same time yearning for the hot lust of Pan's sinewy body.

Without warning, suddenly a large round object was hurtling towards David. An automatic reflex made him reach out to catch whatever it was being apparently thrown at him and his hands gripped the steering wheel of his hatchback; he was driving down the road to the town. He didn't know how he had driven whilst in his dream but somehow had managed. The roads were very wet, it had been one hell of a storm. But now the sun shone on the glaring black tarmac and caused a fierce glare. David's heart was beating fast and he realised how dangerous an experience he just had. He was already slowing the car before he saw the figure standing at the roadside. It was Catherine, naked and looking very, very wet. Braking fiercely, he pulled up and Catherine walked slowly toward the car. Her wet body looked silver in the sunshine. Blinking his eyes and pinching himself didn't help; he wasn't dreaming any longer, this was real. He stretched over and opened the passenger door for Catherine to get in.

"The weirdest things have been happening," they both chorused at once and laughed almost hysterically.

David didn't start the car, but sat still, staring at Catherine, naked and facing him in the passenger's seat. Her eyes told him of Pan and the thrusting and melding and coming. The look of peace on Catherine's face he had only seen briefly before, for fleeting moments of happiness, during orgasm. Now it looked as permanent as anything in this ever-changing world. Perhaps more permanent. It was Catherine who broke the spell. "I'm a little cold, Dave, she said gently, "can we drive on?"

David came back to his senses. Catherine had made an understatement: she was shivering all over, every inch of her body was goose-bump prickly. Her skin looked a shade of night sky blue. Pulling his overcoat from the back seat, David wrapped it around Catherine and tucked her in. Strangely, despite its cold appearance, her body burned his fingers with its fiery heat when his hand brushed her leg. Turning on the engine, he accelerated towards home. He turned to look momentarily at Catherine: her eyes shut, her lips parted, she looked the picture of serenity, except where an almost frothy white saliva dribbled from her lips and over her chin.

The two miles or so to their cottage took longer than it could 'really' have done, or so it seemed to David. And whose black, American limousine-style car was parked out front? It wasn't a good time for visitors so, as he drew up behind the limousine, David planned to get rid of them immediately, whoever they were. He and Catherine needed rest and togetherness, time to recover and share.

A man dressed entirely in black stepped out of the black car. With his back to them, they couldn't see his face but he looked too tall and somehow 'unhuman'. David felt his whole body quiver.

"Dave," Catherine said in a soft, whisper. Just one word, his name, said in such a way David knew just what she meant.

He hadn't switched off the engine. He experienced a coolness and clarity in his mind about what to do next. Sliding the gear lever forward, he automatically released the clutch and accelerated. The car sped forward, down the lane beyond their cottage and towards the sea. It was only a matter of seconds – David was still in third and accelerating fast, but glancing in his review mirror he could see the black car behind. Just before the bend, he saw there were two of them in the car. Obviously, it was *a trick of the light, but they looked like identical twins. Their car much more powerful and they were gaining.*

A few miles down the lane there was a bend. The black car was about fifty yards behind. David saw their only chance and knew they would have to take it. Realizing his intention, Catherine buckled her seat belt in anticipation. He kept his eyes on the road but felt Catherine was smiling at him. "She's enjoying this," he thought and, as they turned a sharp left bend, he suddenly spun the car round to the right and up onto a bank that led to a field overlooking the sea. Screeching to a halt, David and Catherine waited with bated breath. The black car seemed to never arrive then it sped past the track's entrance and they heard it accelerate round and out of the bend.

"They'll soon realise," said David, as he quickly reversed the car out of the track, now facing back in the opposite direction. He felt they now had a chance; the driver of the black car couldn't turn for a quarter of a mile or so on the narrow lane. But, as if by some devilish miracle, the black car was again right behind them. They had lost. A confrontation was all that was left. David switched off the engine and opened his door. The two men dressed in black were already getting out of their car.

It just goes to show you never know what is going to happen next; as true in real life as for these characters. Like all people we meet in life and have relationships with – family, loved ones, friends, and so on – they may come and they equally may go.

This time I guess we will really never know what happened next to David and Catherine. Let's be honest, it's sometimes better not to know.

Surrender

1. The Slave

Mark is a good therapist and dedicated to his work but he met his match with Jon. Jon was devoted to devotion and especially to what he called 'the Goddess'. When Mark first met him, Jon said that he was a slave to 'Her' with a big emphasis on the capital H. Every time he described Her, he would pronounce the word as if it had a capital. You could hear it and, if you didn't, he made sure you knew it was there by forming a large capital H in the air, waving his right hand in a flamboyant way – two down strokes then a swish of a cross bar between them. Mark was never sure if Jon did this intentionally or not but guessed it may have started that way and then grew into a habit, an exaggerated habit at that.

Jon was such a gentle man that Mark felt okay that he exhibited some unusual mannerisms, and, indeed, he found them endearing. About thirty years old, Jon was quite short and had grown his blond hair down to his shoulders. He didn't hold himself well, though, and often looked slumped and lacking physical tone. Mark soon realised how Jon's deep devotion to the Goddess was ruling his life. As their meetings increased, this became all the more apparent. Opening up to Mark, trusting him a little more each time, Jon first appraised Mark of the intense depth of this devotion when he told him that his slavery to Her, as he called it, made him act out in possibly dangerous ways. Mark had an inkling that Jon might be a suicide risk when he described one such incident.

"I was out walking somewhere along the bank of the River Purce," he explained, "and I approached an old log bridge. It was very wobbly, made as it was from two roughly hewn planks. It was one of those damp days when everything was deep green and felt sodden with the heavy rains we've been recently having. The planks that made up the bridge itself looked as if they were soaking wet and, as I walked across, I felt it was time for me to truly dedicate myself to Her."

Mark was curious and asked Jon to tell him what had happened.

"I was calmly balancing myself in the middle of the planks. They were really bending in the middle with my weight, creaking loudly and it felt like they could snap at any moment. I was delighted by this. I realised it was a test of my faith. She could hold me safely or let me fall into her arms. The other side of the river had no meaning, nor the side where I had come from. I felt right at the centre of the circle of my life."

Later, Mark felt that perhaps, if he'd been more skilful at that moment, he would have not spoken to express his concern. Jon looked partly crestfallen, partly enraged, at the misunderstanding.

"You just don't get it do you?" He accused Mark with a dismissive wave of his hand. Then he sat more upright and, as he spoke, his voice became strong and clear: "I am her slave, her piteous, hideous slave, hardly worthy of being kicked into the dust and swept away with the rest of her garbage. Her slave to do with as she wills and here I was, in her power, holding me between the two banks, between life and death. I had tried every way to be fully in Her service, to be at Her bidding. I said to Her, again and again, to do with me as she felt fit. Finally, she has responded."

Mark was more cautious and simply asked Jon what he was feeling at that moment.

"I spoke to Her, I told Her I begged Her to look down upon me and bestow Her kindness by not letting me fall." He stopped and laughed, looking into the distance with a strange vacancy of self. "You'll never believe it, but at that moment a pigeon pooped on my head and I knew it was a signal from Her. I was told to walk on and trust, that my days of slavery were complete and that I could now be the servant, to do my utmost at all times to fulfil Her wishes."

"So you completed walking over the bridge?"

"Oh yes!' he exclaimed with glee.

They sat in silence and their time was completed. Jon assured Mark that it had been a great help and that he would be back for their next meeting.

2 The Servant

The next time Mark saw Jon he was eager to tell him of the job he had started as a barman in a nearby restaurant and bar. "I have a uniform to wear, well it's only a jacket really but with dark trousers and a white shirt I look the part, I well and truly do."

As Mark had previously only seen Jon in jeans and sweatshirt, he looked slightly surprised at Jon's keenness over a uniform. Jon picked this up this quickly. "But I've always liked fine apparel," he said insistently, as if Mark had actually questioned it. "Then the world knows the truth of my relationship with my employer, my position and rank. Everyone can see who I serve with loyalty and in return I am given the status of wearing a uniform." He looked at Mark deeply. "You know who my employer is, don't you?"

Mark wasn't quite sure what Jon meant: did he mean the landlady who he was imagining as the Goddess to whom he was so devoted?

"Yes, it's the landlady," he said with exasperation, "but you know me by now and she is the Goddess, Mrs. Jones. She didn't need to employ me. In fact, I think she might have been somewhat concerned because I'm only on a trial period, but she is teaching me the way to serve her as a man." He smiled warmly. "You could say that she is leading me besides the waters of knowing and I humbly but firmly step behind Her, my feet carefully placed in Her tracks, the footsteps of My Lady."

"That's quite poetic," Mark ventured.

Jon laughed. "I haven't been reading the classics for nothing."

They sat awhile in silence, languishing in the fantasy of being guided by a divine presence in the form of a pub landlady. Al least, that was what was on Mark's mind; as for Jon, he was somewhere else, for him, more real.

"I am hers to do with as she wills, for I am nothing but a vassal who serves Her, not because she commands it, but rather because her presence makes these feelings arise in me. It is my will to serve Her for she is a good mistress, my Lady. I am hers and, after another manner, she is mine. It feels so good that I even dare to think that, one day, I might even be allowed to call Her by Her real name."

"Which is?"

"Ah, so perfect. Stella. Couldn't be a more perfect name for the Goddess, could it?"

Mark felt pleased for Jon that he had a job and that he could engage with it so fully through devoting himself to his boss but he felt uncertain that it would last. Still, it was a step away from his previous sense of complete slavery to the Goddess, now at least he was choosing to serve.

3. The Child

Mark guessed they had meandered off the subject when out of the blue Jon blurted out: "She is my mother."

"The Goddess?" Mark suggested, being quite aware of Jon's way of connecting everything back to his obsession.

"No, Mrs Jones!" he exclaimed.

Mark immediately thought that perhaps this was an expression of Jon's dependence. Perhaps it was too quickly focussed within a situation where he could be terribly let down. Mark was not sure how to respond to Jon but simply repeated his assertion with a slightly questioning tone. "Your mother?"

Jon remained quiet for a while, breathing more deeply, then he closed his eyes and spoke in his unexpectedly sonorous voice, his right arm flailing about as he drew in the air the H every time he said 'Her'.

"It is as if I am Her child, Her child who she tends with such loving awareness, Her child who grows in Her image for she has chosen me for the role and and it shall be. Or perhaps I am rather like a favourite offspring in the garden of its mother plant; I am watered, I am sunned, I am fed daily with all the goodness of Her care and attention. When I bloom, in Her eyes, I will be the most beautiful of all Her children."

"Hmmm," Mark ventured, still concerned about Jon's dependence, "I don't think Mrs. Jones will feel she knows you that well yet."

"Not Mrs. Jones," Jon exclaimed. "The Goddess of course!"

4. The Priest

Jon seemed reluctant to tell Mark something he described as 'very important news but very private'. Mark didn't take the bait and said it was up to Jon what he shared. The more Mark resisted wanting to know, as he correctly guessed, the more Jon would finally tell him what it was.

"I've joined a coven," he blurted out. "It's supposed to be a secret."

"I won't tell anyone," Mark said. He wasn't really surprised; it fitted Jon's devotion to the Goddess to want to join a group – a 'coven' – that would support and further his devotional bent. "What kind of coven is it?"

"They made me a priest," he replied.

Mark was silent. He wondered if Jon's response was telling him something because, after all, you wouldn't expect someone to be a priest as soon as they joined any kind of religious or spiritual grouping. They sat quietly for quite a while and the tension was palpable. Finally, Mark broke it with a simple, "yes?"

"Actually, I'm a novice priest really, but I think they know how serious I am and that I've been devoted to the Goddess for so long already. The best bit was the initiation – it culminated in me falling to my knees …" His voice trailed off as his expression turned to one of wonder and delight.

"What happened?"

"Well, there was a ceremony, lights and incense and – you know – and then at the peak of it I had to fall to my knees and, just as I was about to do that, a cloaked figure stepped forward and held me tightly. Then the Goddess spoke to me and said: 'you must not kneel to me or another in supplication, it must be in deep adoration. Are you ready?' I nodded my assent and the cloaked person let me go and I fell quite hard onto my knees and words just flowed out of me."

Mark was impressed, it sounded like an effective ritual and very appropriate for Jon. He let go for that time of his concerns of what sort kind of group Jon had joined. His hope was that it was serious and not some kind of awful cultish thing. "So can you remember what words flowed out of you?" he asked.

"Surely I can," Jon replied, taking a big breath and speaking with his low, sonorous voice. "My Goddess, it is You I adore, I am now your priest, hear my prayer, and for evermore I shall reside in the temple of your love and sing praises to your wondrous being. Oh my Goddess, touch the heart of this your priest with your tender, caressing fingertips; breathe into my head the balmy breezes of your scented breath. Take me as I am, that is, yours alone. There is truly no other Goddess but you, and I am your appointed priest. Amen unto the ages, and unto the ages, and unto the ages."

"Wow! That's very rich and poetic – and you remember it. I'm impressed."

"Yes, I learned it off by heart. The rituals are recorded so I could listen to me saying it over and over afterwards. Great, eh?"

5. The Sibling

After their last meeting, whilst Mark was pleased for Jon that he had found something meaningful for himself and was very clearly very happy – delighted even – with his life now, he couldn't help being worried that after all this Jon might crash. He had a previous history of highs followed by lows so Mark's concerns were not without precedent. When Jon arrived, however, he was still in a happy connected state but what he opened with was a surprise.

"You know,' he said, "you are the only person that truly gets me and I know now why. We were always meant to be meeting like this because you are my brother."

"Yes, in a sense we are all brothers and sisters to one another of course," Mark said, slightly warily.

"Sure, but more than that. You love the Goddess, don't you?"

"I appreciate the Goddess in all her forms, yes," Mark replied.

"And is not the Goddess our mother?"

Mark was now feeling wary and uncertain what was the best course to take but he followed his track of being honest whilst at same time trying to keep it sane. "She is the mother of everyone if you see it that way," he replied, "but we are not actually brothers, not in a physical sense."

"Indeed, of course," Jon responded but in a low, intimate voice just as if he were a brother confiding with his twin brother. "But we two of us are truly one. No, we didn't emerge from the same woman's womb but are we not the same birth children of the Goddess, our mother earth? And shall we not meet in the same death?"

Mark felt concerned where this was heading. He didn't think for one moment that Jon meant they would die together – that is, that somehow he might engineer it so they died together. He didn't think that Jon would murder him, either, but, at the same time, it was concerning that he was now coming to some notion of them dying together.

Jon, with his usual sharpness, picked up Mark's concern. "Don't worry, I mean after we die," he explained, "it's timeless then so we will meet as if it is at the same time." He paused and looked at Mark very strongly with his eyes wide. "I admire you, my brother, as you admire me for we are of the lineage of the Goddess. In the coven rituals I have been shown your role in my life and my role in your life. Do you want to know, too?"

"Hmm, I think some things are better kept as a mystery."

"I respect that then. Let me just say we shall walk ever onwards, together, unattached, but at the same time completely confident in our interdependence."

6. The Friend

Next time, Jon was on a roll. "What is a brother or sister who is not also a friend? And indeed, brother, blood my own, we are truly friends, too, for I aid you and you aid me and we never ask, it is just given."

"That's not strictly accurate," Mark replied. "You don't directly, and your insurance pays me for seeing you."

"Phooey to that! Who do you think you are, my therapist?"

"That's the deal."

"Then you're madder than I thought. I'm outta here." And with that he strode out of the room, noisily stomped through the hall and slammed the door behind him.

7. The Final Step

Jon didn't return for his next appointment. Mark tried contacting him, left messages on his mobile and so on, but Jon didn't contact him back. Mark didn't really know quite how much he had upset Jon, or how exactly, but Jon clearly didn't want to be in contact with him and he had to accept that. Whenever he recalled their contact, however, Mark found himself feeling very warm towards Jon despite the difficulties.

Mark reflected on Jon's progress through the time that he has seen him. At first, Jon described being a slave to the Goddess, besotted with his feelings of being devoted to his Lady, as he called the Goddess at that time. Was it progress when as a servant he drew so close, or imagined himself so close, to Mrs. Jones, the pub landlady where he worked? From a sense of slavery imposed upon him – for who truly chooses to enter slavery? – to being able to take an oath of fealty was most definitely a move in the right direction.

Mark reflected that perhaps he helped Jon separate the idea of being the child of the Goddess from being the offspring of Mrs. Jones; but then perhaps that devotion would have been the right level for him if he had stayed longer. Mark thought that Jon's parent projection had transferred to him and they clung silently together in a dependence of one to another, but then Jon took another step and grew up as it were, taking the role of the priest, again devoting himself to the Goddess.

As the priest, Jon was so happy. One time he actually sang in the session, a song of the adoration he felt for the Goddess who he now believed was truly One with him. Mark guessed that Jon felt he was closer to him when he shifted towards seeing Mark also as a priest then as a sibling. Jon yearned for that tender, confident communion of trusting siblings that Mark couldn't provide. Then Jon tried a conjuration of the comradeship of a friend with a friend and Mark felt it essential to maintain a boundary, though he could have easily been Jon's friend in other circumstances. Slave, servant, child, priest, sibling, friend, six stages of devotion each an evolution from the previous stage. There was only one deeper step possible and years later, out of the blue, Jon came back into Mark's life and brought the missing step with him.

Mark had changed considerably in those years, for not only was he was no longer Jon's psychotherapist, he was no longer practicing. In fact, Jon had been partly responsible for Mark's changing career, being one of several patients whom he realised he had not really completed with and to which he had become too close, too attached. His supervisor assured him this was part of a learning process but Mark couldn't shake off his sense of inadequacy as a therapist. He had a hobby in making fine jewellery out of recycled objects and he realised this would make a better career for him to pursue. He was actually doing quite well and some of his pieces had been entered for a prestigious show. Everything was working out fine and, quite honestly, he didn't miss the weight of carrying other peoples' issues.

Mark always vividly remembered the day Jon unexpectedly arrived at his door. It was a Thursday afternoon in July, about the time he'd had sessions with him five years previously. Mark answered the door and before him stood a magnificent light, a person so bright and engaging it took him a while to recognise Jon. Finally, it dawned on him: "Jon," he blurted out and stood there dumbfounded to see Jon so elegantly dressed, for now he could see that he was wearing a white suit with a deep bright blue shirt underneath, unbuttoned at the top. But it wasn't his clothing that had made Jon shine so much, it was the physique he had developed. Previously he had been a rather scrawny body with poor muscle tone but now he stood tall and commanded attention.

"You going to ask me in then?" Jon asked with a large, toothy smile.

Mark didn't take him into what used to be the consulting

room but through to his studio at the back of the house. They didn't sit, though, Jon walked on through the open back door and into the small garden. Mark followed behind, somewhat bemused, very anxious, but also, he felt, very delighted to see Jon again.

"There is only one more way we can know one another," Jon said, reaching out and holding Mark's hand, "only one more union we can make in this our physical life. Take my heart, you know."

Mark knew then what this had all been leading to, and in that uniting of passion, lover with lover, there was an end that was also a beginning. After all, what else was there to do but to surrender to Love?

Not All Here

Chris the shaman once took me to a special wood. "There's a portal there," he claimed, but wouldn't say more about it when I asked him. "Wait and see."

Of course, expectation and anxiety make any experience more intriguing and exciting, so I purposely took deep breaths and kept myself calm. I tried to stay focused on each step of the journey rather than being concerned about where we headed, a task I found really difficult. To get to the special wood we had to walk a long way, firstly on a well-trodden track and then on a much rougher path which was largely overgrown. It was maybe around ten o'clock at night and the October sky was largely clear, revealing a myriad of stars. A waning quarter moon shone low on the horizon so our way was not well lit. As it had rained earlier, everything was wet and, although the light was poor, drops of glistening water were clinging to the bushes and the leaves had an eerie shine.

As we picked our way along the track to the wood, my eyes accustomed to the lack of light and after a while it didn't seem that dark after all. However, this didn't stop me putting my foot in it – literally. Without warning, my left foot stepped into a deep puddle and, as I fell forward onto my knee, muddy water from the puddle splashed up my trousers, inside and out. I involuntarily let out a cry of surprise.

"Shh, you'll frighten off the entities," whispered Chris, turning his head in my direction and putting a finger to his lips. Wet and wretched, I now felt even more anxious as I wondered exactly what 'entities' Chris was referring to. I didn't need to speak out my concern. "Oh, just some locals," Chris said in a cheery voice, just as if he was referring to some locals in a nice cosy pub rather than out in a damp, wet field in the middle of the night.

We trudged on; well, I trudged on, I don't think Chris trudged at all but strode forward with a strong sense of intention in his steps. Finally, we reached the special wood. I was shivering now, partly from the cold, partly from nerves. The track narrowed and darkened as we went deeper into the wood, then I could see what appeared to be a light emanating from beneath a tree ahead of us. It couldn't be possibly real, yet as we approached closer, it was clear there was a dim but very distinctive glow of light under the low-slung branches of a vast, overgrown hawthorn tree.

Then I could see what appeared to be two eyes staring out from the light; two, as I imagined, eyes of a very frightened animal, more nervous of us than I had been of what it might be. I guessed it must be an animal that had sheltered there to sleep for the night and that we had disturbed it. I wasn't anxious now but became frightened in a deeper, more visceral way. What if the creature was dangerous? It looked threatening as we moved slowly, even closer now, standing side by side only a couple of metres before the strange light with the now glowering eyes. I thought I could almost hear a snarl and was about to turn away when suddenly, unexpectedly, Chris pulled me towards and into the tree.

I found myself standing in a hot, steamy swamp surrounded by giant ferns, damp and glistening. Everything was cloaked in swirls of dripping wet, thick mist. The humidity was high which made it difficult to breathe easily. I felt like I needed to gulp for air but I couldn't seem to get enough air into my lungs to fill them. Each breath felt like a struggle that didn't quite succeed. Sounds of various creatures filled my ears with a cacophony of piercing sounds; kind of like crickets or other similar sounds and maybe frogs croaking, but so loud they filled the air until I felt completely enveloped by the sounds. Mostly, though, it was just such a shock to be in this different space. I couldn't have vomited if I'd wanted to, the air was all too thick. It wasn't that I really needed to, it was more my body's response to this very strange and frightening situation.

Chris walked forward and, without actually looking back, told me to follow him. I say he told me but he didn't speak, it was more that I heard his voice in my head.

"Where are we?" I asked. The words were so difficult to get out I wasn't sure he had heard me, or if my words sounded like gibberish.

"Nowhere out there but everywhere in here," he replied enigmatically.

"What?"

"We're still out there, waiting for us to return." There was a seemingly long silence where his words hung in the air like the mist swirling around us. "It'll be like we were never gone."

I was very nervous already, but somehow his words made me feel panicky. "How long will we be here?"

"Forever."

It wasn't as easy as he made it look as he stepped forward. Each step was such an effort, my legs felt so heavy. At one point Chris told me to look down at my body. To my surprise – although why I felt surprised when everything in this world was so surprising – I was naked, but what I saw hardly looked like me. My body appeared toned, strong with intense musculature and much darker skinned. This was another shock, almost too much

82

for me to bear. I felt like I was losing consciousness.

"No!" Chris commanded, as sudden and sharp as when you're woken from a deep sleep by an alarm clock. "Don't go there, come up with me." So saying, he moved forward as if gliding; his whole body lifted from the ground and moved forward with grace and ease. I tried the same and it worked. I found myself following Chris as we gently glided out of the engulfing mists and towards a beautiful meadow.

It's strange that too much of a good thing can be as overwhelming as dark, difficult things. This was one of those times. After gliding over the meadow, which was richly coloured with an abundance of wild flowers, we landed near to the edge of a wood, but not like the wood where we had been. This was more like the edge of a large, mediaeval forest. The sense was that no human had ever entered its depths which, although dark, were strangely enticing. I heard Chris tell me to just watch and then I had the feeling that he had left me there alone.

The forest was so incredibly green; every shade of green you could imagine, all glowing as if lit by the late afternoon sun. It might have been late afternoon for all I knew, I had no sense of time, wrapped as I was in the warm, golden richness. I was mesmerised and felt so engaged. Time had stopped and nothing existed but me and the forest which now was speaking to me. Of course, not in words, or even in the way I heard Chris's voice in my head. The voice of the forest was all consuming, like when a lover speaks gently and closely to you. I wanted to merge with the forest so much, to become one with it for ever. It was more than love, or maybe less than love, I couldn't say, but it was a deeply seated obsession. It wasn't all about warmth and goodness either; I felt in myself the pain the trees feel as humans ignore their sentience and use and abuse them.

I took one step forward, wobbly, but firmly, the first step on my way to become one with the forest trees, when suddenly I felt a strong pull from behind accompanied by a loud, bellowing, "No!" My whole body shook from soles of my feet right through to the crown of my head. Shocked, I stopped and turned around. It was as if all the meadow flowers, every single one of them, in their multitudinous colours, were telling me, commanding me, not to lose myself in the forest's embrace. Momentarily, I felt split, not knowing which way to go, then I became completely and utterly overwhelmed. I was lost and all this was really too much to bear. Everything started going blank. I felt like I was falling – which I was, back in the wood with Chris, half stumbling, falling over on my right side.

Ever since, it has seemed to me like part of me never left the mediaeval forest. I am still there merged with its deep sense of just being itself. At night, sometimes, I catch a glimpse of its power; yes, I can see it anytime in my mind's eye, but this is with the full feeling lingering over me, enticing me. It keeps me awake, then I sleep, relieved to be both there and here, but not all there. Ever since then, when people suggest I'm not all here, little do they know how right they are.

The Wisdom of the Birds

I was walking over a smallish hill on a very muddy path with Chris the shaman and two others, Johnno, who I was told is a scribe, and Annetta who, well, who remains a mystery. Chris had suggested it or, rather, 'summoned' me to this walk which he said was to nowhere in particular and that it all depended upon 'who fell first.' I had no idea what he meant, but he was often making such incomprehensible statements so I thought little of it. I was just happy to be out with him in nature, expecting something fantastic to happen.

It didn't seem much like that, though, as we were trudging through thick, sticky mud and I was trying to avoid the slippery parts by walking on the bramble and other vegetation alongside the path. The bramble was worst, like coils of razor wire with thorns that tried their best to rip into my flesh, and tentacles that tried to trip me up at every step. It was whilst walking on the edge to avoid mud that I was finally tripped by a long, dangly strand of bramble.

I tried to save myself from falling but, having lost my balance, knew I was going to fall into the mud. Chris reached out very quickly, you'd think to save me, but instead he pushed me over so my whole body fell right into the mud. Just momentarily, I lost consciousness. I didn't understand at the time but I was 'the first to fall.' This event, if you could call it that, was unpredictable; how could it have been otherwise? Yet, on this walk with Chris and the others it was the stated purpose for being there; and, let's be honest, I was clearly the target.

I didn't remember speaking at all when I was apparently unconscious, or so I thought. I only seemed to me to be unconscious for a moment or two. Johnno, however, somehow wrote down all I described during this apparently short episode. Here is what he recounted back to me, reading from a little notebook that he carried everywhere with him. When he finished, he rather dramatically ripped the pages from his notebook and handed them to Chris. I thought I understood his 'role' as a scribe then and more so when Chris handed me the pages later. Johnno's handwriting was very clear but he hadn't used any punctuation, I added that when I typed it up some days later.

"All is black before me and I see a vesica shaped opening to another world. I climb through, the sun is very hot. I look at it and can see the light emanating from it but not the sun itself. I am dressed in tee-shirt and light trousers. There is a stream with a waterfall, with a cave behind it, behind me. In front is a wood, lots of beautiful flowers – particularly red 'honeysuckle' shaped flowers flashing against the green foliage. There is much sound of insects and bees but they are going about their business and don't worry me. I decide to go into the cave and enter the stream and walk up to the waterfall. I stop to enjoy the water rushing all over me, then enter the cave; it is jet black and a perfect sphere. I stay awhile and notice I can see my reflection in the jet although it is pitch black in there. I come out but, before doing so, remove my wet clothes so that I can feel the water all over my body. This is very invigorating. I leave my clothes to dry and walk down the stream to the sea.

"The shore is beautiful and I wade into the water, deeper and deeper. The sea is crystal clear and I can see the bottom, and occasional multi-coloured fish. I go with the tide – which is going out – and merge with the sea. I am the sea. I no longer feel separate, I have merged with an eternal sea. The only thing left is a sound – hshsh haa – very beautiful experience. It is as if I am right on the point where the tide has stopped before turning and going back in. Then it does, and I am washed towards the shore. I go in and out, at times one with the sea, then at times separate. I realise I have to choose to separate and do so, becoming a piece of drift wood washed up on the shore.

"I am lying face down on the beach and the Angel comes in the shape of a beautiful woman with knee length hair. I am shivering cold although the sun is still shining brightly. My physical body is actually shaking all over. The Angel turns me over and I see her eyes – they are the sun. The body of the sun is no longer obscured by its light ... in her eyes I can see the sun itself. I feel healed and energized.

"I stand up and start walking back up the stream. When I reach the trees there is a myriad of different birds singing and all watching me. A blackbird comes and sits on my hand. It looks at me with one yellow eye, his head cocked to one side, and again I can see the sun itself, but now I can see the black hole, the pupil at the centre. The blackbird says this is my soul. It says that black is the colour of the soul because black receives all impressions, is totally absorbing and rejects nothing. I feel one with the blackbird, it merges with me and I continue up the stream.

"A white fan-tailed pigeon appears and, after what the blackbird said, I am interested to find out what a white bird signifies, so ask it. It grows until it is the same size as me then unbuttons its front and out pops a black bird. This then unbuttons its skin and a white bird appears. I see several changes of white to black to white like this until it reaches the very centre from where all of a sudden, a humming bird, multi-coloured and with a long thin beak, flies out. It hovers around my head, humming all the time, then it stops in front of my face and says: if you get confused between polarities and you don't know which is black or white just imagine me humming around your head. Then it 'sort of' smiles at me and flies off.

"I continue up the stream and reach the wood and the waterfall again. My clothes have dried so I put them back on, but now they are the blue shirt and blue jeans I am actually wearing. I see a chameleon on some sand and pick it up and place it on the grass. It turns green to merge with its background then crawls back to the sand, turning sandy coloured again. It says: 'whatever you are like on the outside, the inside is always the same.'

"The chameleon turns into the vesica shaped opening which I came out. I climb through the vesica, and I am back where I started."

I initially believe I can see the countryside surrounding where I'm sitting on a small bank beside a muddy path. Chris, Johnno and Annetta are sitting beside me. And then, as I become more conscious of where I am, I realize we are in Chris's house. We were never in the field! I never slipped in mud, but I know I clearly experienced it happening. Strangely, though, my clothes are clean – if I experienced what I thought I had, surely the front of my clothing would be covered with mud? This made me feel even more confused: were we outside or not? Nothing seemed to add up and I became quite agitated about it. The shaman assured me to trust whatever I had experienced and handed me the script as written by the scribe. It is all there, I know it happened, I know it was a real experience, but there is no actual memory now, just the written script. Chris was very evasive and seemed to suggest we had really been out in the country but when questioned wouldn't say more except repeating the chameleon's words: 'whatever you are like on the outside, the inside is always the same.'

I didn't know what to think: what, if anything, had really happened. My discomfort wasn't helped when Annetta hugged me and laughed and laughed as if it was all the greatest joke ever – or that I was the greatest joker ever. This really annoyed me and I felt even more confused. The angrier and more confused I felt, the more she laughed. I felt like I didn't know anything anymore, apart from one thing: that imagining the humming bird flying around my head really made me feel better. So, I breathed, relaxed, and imagined, no, really felt it as if it was an actual experience. Then I knew it doesn't matter if the experience was real or not. I am soul and I can receive all impressions and reject nothing. I feel more alive than I ever have and the wisdom of the birds has guided me since. And, you know, strange thing was, when I came to leave, my boots were dirty.

✣

Mabel's Mindfulness

Ken didn't know mindfulness could be dangerous until one day several months after he had attended a week-long course, when he happened upon one of the other participants. Mabel was working at the same social services office as Ken, albeit not in the same department. When they bumped into each other in a corridor the recognition was instant although they hadn't really had much, if any, contact on the course.

"Hey, I know you, you were in the training," declared Mabel as she rushed up to Ken and, much to his surprise, gave him a big wet kiss on his cheek. He honestly felt, as he slightly reeled from such an approach, that she would have landed her kiss on his lips if he hadn't managed to turn his face slightly away in time.

"Yes, hi," he replied, trying to not sound discombobulated. He did recognize her, she was quite distinctive with her wild red hair and chubby features. He had no idea who she was though, he didn't even know her name.

"You remember me, don't you?" she asked, a slight tone of pleading in her voice.

"Yes, but I'm useless with names so I can't remember, sorry, but –"

She jumped in, not letting him finish his sentence. "Mabel. I'm Mabel," she almost shouted with a wild laugh. "You can't forget a name like mine!"

Yes I can, thought Ken but, being the polite guy he was, he agreed. "Yes," he said, "of course, I remember now." He paused. She looked at him expectantly, obviously wanting more. He wasn't sure what to say but decided to go for honesty. "We didn't really have that much contact back then."

"But Ken, don't you remember that time you picked me up after I'd slipped on the ice during that really cold spell during the course?"

Ken did remember. He was walking behind a woman he didn't know as she trounced along the pavement seemingly unconcerned about the icy ground. He remembered thinking that she was taking risky steps. In all honesty, when she slipped and fell backwards onto her backside, he thought she somewhat deserved it. He wanted to laugh, probably did inside, but outwardly he was the gentleman as always, offering his help to the woman, assisting her in standing and dusting herself off. She hadn't been hurt at all, or so it appeared, and after a brief exchange they parted. That was it, nothing more, thought Ken, but for Mabel it had been a memorable event.

"Oh yes," she said quickly, "I had a big bruise on my bum for ages afterwards. I've got a picture of it. I'll show you sometime." She hardly noticed as Ken reacted to this idea somewhat negatively. He felt sure he didn't want to see any such picture. "Oh yes, you'll be amazed how big it is. But it would have been worse if you hadn't rescued me."

"I hardly rescued you."

"Oh, but you did, not just helping me up, you were kind and concerned. It made me realize how important the training was for us; how we were good people and only someone with the level of consciousness you get from the training would have been so helpful."

Now Ken realised she was off on one. He most certainly didn't want to go down that track. Already taking a dislike to her, he couldn't see how what she was saying had any relevance. The mindfulness training wasn't why he helped her, but, if she thought that, it was her business not his. He smiled a lot and excused himself, saying he was very busy and had to get on.

"I look forward to seeing more of you, then," she said eagerly, making as if she was about to plonk another kiss on his other cheek. Ken managed to avoid that by a quick sidestep then immediately regretted answering, "Yes, of course, maybe we can have a drink sometime."

Mabel came looking for Ken the next day and before he had a chance to say yes or no, Mabel asserted her will. There was no 'sometime' for her; she assailed Ken with her demand: "Tonight then. I'm not taking no for an answer, I owe you – and hey, we're already friends, aren't we?"

"Ah, yes, sure," replied Ken, not really certain how to proceed. Following something he had picked up on the course, he decided that honesty would be the best policy. "But I'm a family man, Mabel, and I have two young children, Tom and Tina. They're twins, they're only four, and after work I like to go home to them, spend time with them before their bedtime. You understand, don't you?"

"Of course, but I'm only suggesting a quick drink – not a shag!"

Taken aback by her forwardness, Ken almost blushed, or at least he felt like he did. "No, no, I'm not saying that," he countered. "I'll talk to Paula and see if I can arrange it."

"You have to ask your wife if you can go out?" Mabel responded somewhat aggressively.

Ken felt annoyed now. "Listen, Mabel, my wife has been with the twins all day long and I want to give her a break for an hour or two before we put them to bed. I do it because I love her and care – and, as I said, I want to spend time with my children."

So saying, he went to walk away, he didn't want her to see how upset she was making him, but Mabel wasn't having any of that. Grabbing his arm, she leant into his space and said: "One drink, that's all. Dangerous or dead!" Before he could say anything, she trounced off.

Ken was upset all day by this and decided he needed to put Mabel straight. Just because they'd both been on the same mindfulness course did not mean they were inevitably friends. When by chance – or was it? – he bumped into her not long before the end of the work day, he was ready. "You got time after work tonight?" he asked.

"Yes," she replied, not disguising her pleasure at his suggestion.

"One drink at the local wine bar and we can talk some, ok?"

"Yes, yes. Sure, one drink, that's great. I'll see you out the front just after five then."

Ken wasn't sure he was doing the right thing. He phoned Paula to tell her he was having an after-work meeting with a colleague. He didn't mention it was a female colleague, or that it was at the wine bar, not because he was hiding anything, but because he didn't want to worry her. Paula sounded fine about it anyway. She encouraged him, saying he needed to get out with his colleagues more and have a break after work sometimes before the intensity of home life.

The wine bar meeting went quite differently than Ken intended. The biggest shock for him was how much he enjoyed the time with Mabel. How interesting – and interested – she was. They laughed a lot, especially over their second and third drinks, about the teacher and other students on the course they had both attended. In fact, Ken so lost track of time it was Mabel who finally suggested he should go home. They ended the evening with a brief A-frame hug and lots of warm exchanges about meeting up again. By the time Ken got home the children were already in bed. Paula was very happy he'd obviously had a pleasant outing.

"You deserve it," she insisted as they snuggled together on the sofa. She suggested that Ken invite Mabel round for dinner one evening. "We've hardly seen any dinner guests since before the kids," she said. "It would be nice to do some more entertaining again."

Ken wasn't so sure about asking Mabel for dinner, but he didn't express his doubts to Paula. Although he had a great, fun evening with her, he also noticed how Mabel, as he put it to himself, 'held the floor.' Lying in bed later, his mind still racing, he realised that most of their exchanges had been either about Mabel or her telling him what he should or shouldn't be doing. He could recall two occasions when she cut through whatever he was saying to share something else to do with her. 'Very self-centered person,' he reflected. 'I'm not sure I really like her enough to want her here.' But he wondered if he was being silly, judgmental even. 'After all, it was only one meeting, we were both excited and it was fun.' He also realised from their sharing that it appeared Mabel had a much more interesting life than him.

The following day at work Ken only saw Mabel once. He was in meetings most of the time and she was in another department. Just as he was leaving, she popped up and he was greeted again by one of her wild kisses, this time landing right on his lips. He wanted to wipe his lips but felt that would be too rude. He told Mabel that Paula had suggested he invite her round for dinner.

"That will be fantastic," said Mabel, obviously delighted at the idea. Fumbling in her shoulder bag, she pulled out a rather battered looking iPhone and suggested they make the date now. Ken thought this far too quick and said he had to be somewhere and hadn't time to arrange it then. "At least give me your address," she said, opening her contacts app, "and I'll be able to look where you live and plan how I'll get there when I visit."

Somewhat reluctantly, he agreed and gave her his address and mobile number which she eagerly entered into her contacts. It all seemed satisfactory and Ken wasn't fazed. He knew he would have to invite her but there was no rush.

Ken couldn't possibly have predicted what happened next. About nine o'clock, Paula and he had put Tim and Tina to bed and were settling down to watch some tv when there was a ring at the door. When Ken went to see who was calling at such an hour, to his surprise it was Mabel. "Hello," she said, smiling widely, "I was passing in the area so I thought I'd just drop in, on the off chance, as it were." Before Ken could decide if it was ok or not, Mabel was already entering the house, giving him, not the expected attempt at a big kiss, but just a slight hug. "Wow, you've a lovely house!" she exclaimed, now over the threshold.

Paula came to see what was happening. "This is Mabel," said Ken, somewhat limply. He felt unwelcoming: he hadn't planned this and he didn't want it to be happening. Mabel was already greeting Paula, making a big fuss of how she was so lovely and what a big smile she had. Paula invited Mabel right in and offered her some tea.

"And a biscuit if you've got one," said Mabel, "I'm feeling famished."

"We've got some left-over dinner, if you like," Paula said kindly. "It's not much, only a pasta dish."

Mabel happily agreed and before Ken knew what was happening, she was sitting on the sofa balancing a plate of pasta salad on her lap and eagerly eating. It wasn't like Ken really minded, it was more that he hadn't invited her and he didn't like uninvited guests, whoever they were. But, at the same time, he felt mean, especially compared with Paula's kindness. He decided to let go of his negativity. Paula and Mabel seemed to have hit it off and were sharing things about their lives, what they were into and stuff. When Mabel had finished her food, he took her plate to the kitchen, offering to make tea for everyone.

It was when he came back with the drinks that things started to get weird. Mabel was speaking enthusiastically about the mindfulness training where she had met Ken and he heard her say: "Ken was easily reprogrammed, a very easy subject."

"What did you say?" he asked, shocked not only at what she was saying, but that it didn't make any sense. It had been a mindfulness course and had nothing to do with programming, or reprogramming, or anything like that.

"Oh you know, on day two when you were chosen to be the one out the front of the group. You got it straight away. it only took a few minutes to reprogramme you."

"But that wasn't reprogramming," Ken insisted. "It was just an exercise in self-awareness and self-consciousness. Being in front of others and having to speak."

"Yes, exactly. You were being programmed to neuro-linguistically respond to certain triggers and not to others. That is how the master teaches it."

What master?" Ken sounded incredulous. "You mean Guy who ran the group?"

"Of course. And mindfulness is only a small part of his spiritual programme. Guy is an ascended master, you know."

Ken was now getting agitated by Mabel again. Guy had seemed like a nice but pretty straightforward bloke to him, certainly not an 'ascended master' whatever that meant.

"You signed up for the next course, didn't you?" asked Mabel.

"In principle, yes, but I wasn't actually planning on doing it, it's not..."

Mabel keenly interrupted him. "But you have to, you are part of our group now. We need you there."

"Poppycock!" exclaimed Ken, visibly irritated by what Mabel was asserting. He was upset by the idea he would have anything to do with what was now starting to sound like a cult.

"Ken," warned Paula, "don't get so worked up, it's a simple misunderstanding, I'm sure." At the same time, she was trying to communicate to him non-verbally that Mabel was a guest and he shouldn't be rude.

"I'm sorry," said Mabel. "It's late and I should be off anyway. It's so lovely to see your house and meet you, Paula. What a wonderful life you have." Ken was still seething inside but was starting to relax when she added, "Now it would be great to meet your children."

Before Ken could say anything, Paula responded very positively. "Oh yes, you must," she said. "What about coming round Friday after work? I can make us a nice meal, not this left-over stuff, and you'll meet Tim and Tina."

Mabel was so keen, Ken couldn't say anything. She then left pretty quickly with only a minimum hug with him and what he thought was an over-indulgent, long and close hug with Paula.

Once she was gone, Paula challenged Ken. "What was that all about then?" she asked strongly. "Mabel seems like a really nice, friendly person."

Ken was tired and grumpy and told his wife he was too tired to talk about it and would continue the conversation tomorrow. He genuinely felt tired, but nevertheless found it hard to sleep at all, so much was going round in his mind. For a start, the mindfulness training hadn't been a cult or anything. Guy was not a guru, and there was certainty nothing spiritual about the course. Ken avoided spiritual things like the plague. But he couldn't help wondering about Mabel. He considered whether maybe he fancied her, but felt sure he didn't, she just wasn't his type with her thick, glowing red hair and her girly, rounded face. But then he stopped himself. It didn't matter whether he fancied her or not; he didn't, but anyway he was a happily married man who loved his wife. All these thoughts went through his mind and deeply disturbed his rest. He was tired the next day and hated the idea of bumping into Mabel but thankfully didn't. He decided that he would be nice, be kind, she could come to dinner once and meet the twins. Beyond that he'd make sure the contact tailed off to nothing. He really didn't like her and certainly didn't want her in their life.

Friday, the day of the dinner, came and Ken felt disturbed all day, wishing Mabel wasn't coming to dinner, and worse, coming directly after work so she could meet the children. He hadn't spoken much about it to Paula. She had dismissed his concerns as nonsense and said it was good to have a potential new friend who was such a nice person. Ken didn't say any more. He was coping with it, though, even when he bumped into Mabel in a corridor and she told him she was leaving work early that day so she could go home to prepare for what she called 'the big evening.' She even tried to move in for the lip kiss even in the corridor at work. Ken wasn't having any of that and managed to side step her move and say breezily, "see you later."

"Alligator," she responded gleefully as she bounced off.

Paula spent most of the day preparing some of her favourite recipes. She wore one of her best dresses and, on this rare occasion, put on make-up. Tim and Tina were dressed in their smart clothes and acting a bit manic, knowing something unusual was happening. Ken, on the other hand, hardly had time to turn around when Mabel was already at the door, and what a sight she was. Wearing the shortest mini skirt Ken had ever seen – well, for years anyway – and a blouse that was tight enough to emphasise her ample breasts, Ken's first thought was that she looked cheap but then felt guilty for having such a thought. He hadn't time to reflect on this anyway, because Paula was already complementing Mabel on her outfit and how 'fresh and attractive' she looked.

'Fresh and attractive,' thought Ken, 'my foot!' Still, he decided his attitude wasn't warranted. He was being unfair to Mabel; she was just being friendly after all. They attended the same course and, although he couldn't quite place why, he nevertheless felt some allegiance, an affinity with her because they had both been through the same process.

"You seem rather distant," Paula told him as they watched Mabel introducing herself to the twins by dropping down on the floor with them and immediately engaging in some fun horse-play. The kids squealed with delight and clearly loved Mabel already, she was like one of them. Ken hadn't got anything to say to Paula, but he tried to stop analysing everything and just relax into the evening. He couldn't help noticing Mabel's now rather exposed legs as she tumbled about on the floor. He decided he would be better off in the kitchen helping Paula with the meal.

Tim and Tina went to bed happily, if somewhat over-energised. Paula – thankfully, thought Ken – declined Mabel's offer to go up with them. The dinner was delicious, the conversation was friendly and engaging and the wine flowed freely. Ken had completely let go of his concerns and was having a good time. That was until Mabel, getting up to go to the bathroom before leaving, stumbled slightly, and then laughed a lot as she fell into a nearby armchair. "I'm so drunk!" she declared.

Ken had actually not drunk very much and felt fine to drive. He started to offer Mabel a lift home, it would be easy, but Paula interrupted him, eagerly offering Mabel a bed for the night. "We've a spare room, it's made up already, it's no trouble, and you haven't work tomorrow, it's the weekend."

Mabel readily agreed and was very quiet as she sat in the chair watching Ken and Paula clear up and prepare for bed. Paula showed her to her room, gave her a new toothbrush and a large towel, and they all went to bed. Mabel refused the offer of a nightdress with a breezy, "I never wear anything in bed anyway."

"It wasn't so bad after all," thought Ken as he climbed into bed beside Paula. At least now he was having a bit of peace and quiet. Being with Paula in their own space was what he really liked best. Then a little tap on the door was followed by it opening and Mabel's head sticking round the door.

"Good night, thank you again," she said lightly. Ken could see her bare shoulder where it was poking round the door and couldn't help wondering if she was naked. Then Mabel sort of winked at them, kind of without winking, he wasn't sure what she did exactly, and asked, "Want a threesome?"

Both Ken and Paula were shocked when she said this. Ken didn't really know what to say. Of course, he wanted to say no but he found it very difficult to get the word out. He knew he didn't want to share his and Paula's bed with Mabel, however interesting the proposition might be, but he realised something made it difficult, nigh impossible to say no to her. Rather feebly he muttered: "Not tonight, Mabel."

She laughed loudly. "I was only kidding," she exclaimed. "Nighty night, you two." Turning as she closed the door, she gave them a quick view of her back and bottom. Ken's question was answered; she was naked.

After she left, Paula and Ken both sighed with relief and laughed nervously. "She was joking, wasn't she?" asked Paula.

"I don't know," replied Ken, "I don't want her in our house, really."

"Oh c'mon," Paula responded, "she's good fun." Ken looked at his wife incredulously, he wasn't finding Mabel's presence fun at all. "Anyway," said Paula, snuggling closer to him, "it doesn't stop us having a twosome."

There was part of Ken that wanted to say "Not tonight, Paula," just as he had said to Mabel and turn over to sleep, but another part of him rose up with a quite different response. "Yes, let's to it," he declared keenly and, moving closer to Paula, he touched and stroked her body.

Paula was very pleased; they were both tired a lot and hardly made time for sex. She was also surprised at Ken's keenness, all things considered. She engaged with Ken, eagerly removing his pyjamas whilst kissing him passionately. "Mabel seems a good influence on us," she thought as Ken eagerly kissed her.

When they rose in the morning, they found Tim and Tina were up and dressed – something unheard of – and Mabel was gone. A note on the kitchen table thanked them for a wonderful evening. The children were full of how she made their breakfast and helped them get dressed. They were not wearing the most suitable clothes for a Saturday playday but it didn't really matter. The twins went on about how Mabel was the best auntie they had ever had by a million, billion miles.

"She isn't really your auntie," Ken tried to explain but the twins were too young to understand. 'It's like Mary bloody Poppins or something,' Ken grumbled to himself as he ate his muesli. 'Thank goodness she's gone anyway; I won't be inviting her again if I can help it.' His plan was thwarted, however, about half an hour later, when Mabel returned. Refreshed, and dressed in casual clothes, she declared she wanted to give them a wonderful day to repay them for such a good evening. Ken tried putting her off by saying they already had plans, but Paula keenly invited Mabel to spend the day with them.

By lunchtime Ken really had had enough. As he saw it, Mabel spent the morning not giving them anything back, as she had suggested she wanted to do. Instead, she spent the time regaling Paula with stories of how the 'reprogramming', as she called it, had affected Ken. She was making up all sorts of outlandish lies to make him look foolish. Ken played with the twins who, like him, seemed deflated that their new 'auntie' was more interested talking to mum rather than playing with them.

At one point, as he was passing the table where the two women were sitting, he overhead Mabel telling Paula a tale involving him with his trousers off. This was just too much; his reticence to speak up completely broke. "Mabel!" he exclaimed. "That's just not true. Most of the stories you are telling Paula are not true. I never had my trousers off in any group situation, you never saw me without trousers. Why are you saying this?"

"If it's not true," she countered, "how would I know you were wearing red underpants then?"

Ken felt his face reddening. She was right about his unusual choice of coloured pants, yet he also knew she was lying. "I dunno," he tried to explain, "you must have glimpsed them somehow. Anyway, that's not the point, I just know that–"

He didn't finish his sentence. Mabel and Paula were now laughing at him and his embarrassment. He imagined Mabel was turning Paula against him and he didn't feel there was anything he could do. His rage grew and he blurted out: "I want you to leave." And a second time, very loudly: "I want you to leave."

Paula looked shocked: "Ken," she started to interject but he was having none of it.

"I mean it ..." he said and then, backing off because he felt a strange pain in his head and didn't feel quite well, added "... well, after lunch we need space."

"That's fine," said Mabel, still laughing, "I was planning to go before lunch, actually."

Ken's relief to hear this was palpable. He walked through to the kitchen. Paula followed him and started telling him how rude he was being. Mabel hadn't meant any harm, she liked her, and he needed to get his act together. Feeling tongue-tied, he shrugged and went to join the children playing in the garden even though he felt in no mood for playing.

As she was leaving through the garden, Mabel approached Ken. "Do you remember Guy's parting words to you, Ken?"

Her question caught Ken off-guard and he actually thought about it. "Yes," he replied, "what about it?"

"What did he say?"

"Something like the old saying: 'nothing ventured nothing gained' I think," replied Ken honestly.

"Almost," Mabel said, laughing. Then, leaning in close to Ken, she whispered: "dangerous or dead, Ken. Dangerous or dead." She gave him a big smile, then walked off. Ken felt a momentary annoyance but, just as he felt that, at the same moment part of him disagreed. Mabel had somehow opened him up to something, something he couldn't quite remember but something at the core of his being. He realised that Mabel was right, you have to take risks or your life becomes nothing. Dangerous or dead indeed. More than that, he felt strong like never before. He didn't know why he chose this analogy but he told himself it was like being the captain of the ship. He realised how wise Mabel's words were and sensed a new way of seeing the world. Her words hit just the right spot.

Paula was still angry at him when he went inside and ignored his presence. He let her be, then, seizing a moment when the twins were not around, he gently but firmly sat her down on their sofa. "Okay", he said, "I know I've been out of order but I felt a sense that Mabel was trying to harm me, or us."

Paula made to object: "Listen, Ken, she was..." but Ken stopped her.

"I know," he continued, "it was all inside me, I get that. I do think Mabel could be a dangerous influence on us but in fact she has done us so much good. I say 'us' but it is me really. I have been hanging my feelings up and ignoring them whilst plodding on in a job I don't like and–"

Paula continued his sentence: "– and in a relationship you don't like..."

"Not at all!" exclaimed Ken, gently pulling her closer to him. "No, not at all, Paula. I love you unconditionally and endlessly, you know that. I could never do anything to harm that, it is central to my life. You – and the children – are my life. No, the point is Mabel challenged me. I don't know if she knew what she was doing but she challenged me to remember I am the captain of the ship of my life, I can make choices; I am not a victim to circumstances."

Paula didn't immediately get what he was saying. "And me and the children?" she asked.

"You are my co-captain."

"Not just the first mate then?"

"Not at all. In fact, you are not the co-captain, you are the admiral!" Ken exclaimed.

They both laughed a lot and the ice between them was broken. Paula now responded to his embrace and, moving in closer, responded warmly. "And Tim and Tina?" she asked.

Ken thought for only a moment. "Of course, they are the first class, five-star passengers on this ship and we make sure they get all they want."

"But not going overboard, eh?" Paula laughed.

"Better not. But sometimes I do feel like making them walk the plank."

At that moment the twins came back in the room. Life was back to normal only more so. Even the children noticed a new energy about their father and started listening to what he told them more seriously. When bed time came, they hugged him tighter than ever.

Ken and Paula had a serious discussion before the weekend ended about Ken's job and its soul-destroying nature. They agreed that he should give his notice in and start his own consulting business. He had all the necessary skills and contacts, he just never had the confidence before. Monday morning, when he gave in his notice, his boss said she wasn't surprised. He then went off to the department Mabel worked in to find her, apologize and arrange another meeting. To his surprise, he discovered that she had only been a temp. She had finished there at the end of the previous week. They weren't sure where she went next.

She never let on to Ken that she was a temp nor that she was finishing work at his office. He dialed her mobile number several times but there was a message saying the number was out of use. He realised he had no other way of contacting her. He never knew her address, had no idea where she lived, and without the mobile number she was unreachable. There was no link he could find to her on the internet, either. She was gone. Ken felt momentarily anxious then he realised it was as it was: she had been a catalyst in his and Paula's life and he thanked her for that. Indeed, she had disrupted their routine, made them realize just how much they enjoy being a couple, not just any couple but the couple they are with their quirks and idiosyncrasies. It made them stronger and gave the children a firmer base from which to grow.

Part of Ken was kind of glad, he realised, that he wouldn't have to be challenged by her again. "Once is enough," he mused, smiling to himself as he planned his next move toward his new life.

That night, as she snuggled up to Ken after the twins were in bed, Paula commented that Mabel was like an angel breezing through and blowing away their cobwebs. Ken agreed, he liked the metaphor, and, for the first time in years, he led Paula upstairs to bed without having cleared away the dishes and filled the dishwasher.

Mabel was back at work temping elsewhere in a different office. Her neighbour at the next desk was a young Asian man called Rishi. Rishi had attended a one-week course on mindfulness. The recognition was instant although they hadn't really had much contact on the course.

"Hey, I recognize you, you were in the training," declared Mabel as she rushed up to Rishi and, much to his surprise, gave him a big kiss on his cheek.

❖

The Magician's House

Tom liked to walk around the town where he lived, exploring areas he hadn't previously been to or even known of their existence. One such area was a large empty square, not really empty exactly, but full of the debris that such a large empty space accumulates over time. He found this square fascinating and wondered about its history. He could have looked it up on the internet but that would have spoiled his fun and the sense of adventure that went with making up stories for himself. "The actual history would be a lot more boring than what I imagine," he thought as he ambled about the square, turning over upturned boxes strewn in one area to see if anything interesting was inside. There wasn't; there never really was, but that didn't deter him from continuing to look.

He also enjoyed studying the front of the few houses that still stood on the north side of the square and which were occupied by a mix of different types of people as you might expect in a run-down area like this. He experienced hostility from some of these people, but generally they ignored him as he peered into their front yards or stared endlessly at the grand houses, as they had once been. It was hard to believe, but he knew it was true, that some of these houses that were lived in now by several families, each was once owned by a single family, undoubtedly with a retinue of servants. What was the square like in those days? "Certainly not as bleak, nor the wind-attracting dump for all kinds of debris that it was now," he mused as he strode across the square from one side to the other side.

What fascinated Tom most was the large old house and garden that occupies almost the whole of the southern side of the square. Actually, the front of the large, old house and its entrance was round the corner. What interested him most of all was the long, high old stone wall that enclosed the garden and stretched along the square. The wall, about eight feet high, gave a definite 'keep out' message. Tom walked its length many times, running his fingers along the blackened stones from which the wall was constructed. He reckoned that it must have been built when the square was fully occupied, or even before, it seemed so old.

On several occasions he asked one of the occupants of the square if they know anything about it but they always appeared nervous and ignored his questions. They avoided eye contact and looked at him with puzzlement as if it was really weird for him to ask about the house. One old woman told him that it was a magician's house before she turned up her collar and retreated as if from a cold chill, even though the day was sunny and wind free. He thought he heard her mutter 'you know him' as she shuffled off. This intrigued him as he clearly did not. The more he wondered, the more he traced the contours of the wall, the more he discovered people didn't want him asking questions about it let alone to give him any answer. This just fed his fascination with the old house.

So, one day Tom decided he would climb up onto the wall and look over into the garden. The tall wall wasn't an easy climb, especially as its stone bricks, that probably were quite rough initially, had been smoothed off by the elements over many years. It was difficult to find any foothold by which he could hoist himself up. He liked a challenge and this was a great one: how could be look over the wall? A plan was quickly in his head. He would collect together, over a few days, several old boxes and various other rejected items in the square that he could place near the wall without anyone really noticing. If they did, he reckoned, they'd think nothing of it, they were used to his weird behaviour. Then, on a future day, he could pile it high in one spot and use it to climb up and look over the wall.

Finally, the day of action came and his plan worked perfectly. A few old boxes, some rather heavy rocks, and a wooden pallet offered him the required height and was built against the wall in a matter of moments. Tom chose late evening when he knew from experience there were very few people around. He was such a familiar figure in the square by now that even if anyone saw him no one would care what he was doing. With some trepidation and a lot of excitement, Tom climbed on his structure and raised himself right up onto the top of the wall so he could see into what he now called, lightheartedly, 'the magician's garden.'

He didn't feel so lighthearted about it, however, when he looked into the garden because it emanated a dark foreboding. Breathing deeply and slowly, he calmed his nerves. He knew there was nothing to worry about; even if the owners of the house saw him, the worst that could happen would be they would tell him to get off their wall and go away. But all this left his mind as he became more and more entranced by the garden beneath him. It was late evening but the light in the garden seemed darker than it was on the outside. Long and quite thin, the garden stretched right to the back of the house where, he was pleased to notice, no lights were on so, presumably, no one was home.

Tom was frustrated by what he could see down in the garden. There were some bushes, a flower bed, an unusual looking statue near a small pond, but none of this satisfied his curiosity. He knew he had to lower himself into the garden for a closer look around and, as it appeared no one was home, he felt safe doing just that. A convenient water barrel gave him the step he needed to climb down safely, supported, as he did so, by holding onto the long branch of an old, gnarled apple tree.

It was easier than expected and, before he knew it, he was standing on the grass in the magician's garden. He felt his heart beating fast, he was very nervous. He knew he was imagining it, that it was an irrational fear, but he couldn't help feeling that he was being watched. Ignoring these feelings and breathing deeply again, he decided to go towards the statue and the pond. It was the most eerie looking part of the garden and, as the statue appeared to be so unusual, he wanted to see what it depicted. His legs felt a little heavy as he lifted them over a small picket fence carefully placed around the grass, and onto a pebble path that led to the pond.

That's when it happened. Feeling his dread suddenly escalate and a weird buzzing starting in his head, he thought he saw the statue move. A moment later he saw it actually was moving and coming towards him. He wanted to scream but couldn't. He felt rooted to the spot. The mysterious statue was now like a dark enveloping presence that held Tom by his hands, his fingers interlocking with the energy strands emanating from the amorphous blob of terror before him. Somehow he managed to pull his hands away from the creature, turn and run towards the wall. He couldn't remember exactly how it happened, it must have been the fear giving him extra strength, but he found himself right on the top of the wall.

Momentarily breathing a sigh of relief, letting air out from his chest where he had been holding his breath, he turned to look behind him and immediately wished he hadn't. The dark, terrible presence was right there with him. He now screamed and screamed as he tried to pull himself away from the creature. They were locked in a battle of strength or, more truthfully, a battle of wills as to whether he would return into the garden – to what? To be consumed? It was too terrible to contemplate what it might mean to be dragged back. He had to break free and leave the garden for good. Summoning all his energy, he resolved to make a final push for freedom. He had never previously realised how strong he could be, nor acted upon this strength, but this felt like a matter of life and death no less. The next thing he knew was that he was lying on top of his boxes and pallet, crying like a child, shivering, feeling really unwell. Dragging himself up, he scarpered as fast as his legs could take him, away from the square, away from the magician's garden forever.

It took Tom several weeks to recover from his experience. He kept trying to convince himself it had all been a dream. Maybe the pile of boxes he had created had collapsed, he had been knocked unconscious and dreamt the whole thing. Two things convinced him it had been real, though; the absolute terror he had felt which still made his body involuntarily shiver if he spent too long focusing on it, and the fact that when he arrived home that evening, he found strange burn marks on his hands where he had been held by the creature. They disappeared after a day or two but one of his fingers seemed permanently bent out of shape and he was sure it hadn't been like that before.

He didn't really know what to make of it, but decided that the creature must have been some kind of guardian left in the garden by the magician who owned the house to protect it from intruders. He knew this seemed far-fetched, ridiculous even, but he had experienced what he had experienced, there was no doubt about that. The more he mulled it over, which he endlessly did, the more he knew he must go back to the square and ... and what? He didn't know. His resistance to ever going near there again was so strong: for weeks he was sure he couldn't, wouldn't, do it. Then, one evening, his curiosity, his sense of just having to know what it was, got the better of him and he found himself, standing in the square near to the walled garden.

Some of the boxes and the pallet Tom had used to climb were still near the wall but looked like they had been deliberately dismantled to discourage anyone trying to use them as he had. Leastwise, that's what he imagined as he scouted around, not that he had any intention to going up the wall again. He decided that his only course of action now was to go round to the front door, announce his presence to whomsoever answered the door ,and ask them about their house and garden. Not mentioning his experience, of course, he would find out all he could about the place and its owner, the 'magician' as they were called by the old lady that he spoke to all those weeks before. He knew it was a dangerous course of action but felt he just had to know who this magician was with a powerful guardian in the garden.

Slowly and deliberately, breathing carefully to stop himself panicking, Tom walked round the corner and came to a small yard in front of the main door of the house which, much to his surprise, was open. It looked quite light and inviting but he wasn't about to go inside, not after his last experience. If they had such a guardian in the garden what might happen if he dared enter the house? He tapped on the door and no one came. He tapped louder and then a third time louder still. No one answered. Tom daringly decided to step just inside the hall. The door would be open behind him and he could make a quick escape if needed. He called again and took one step right towards the door, another call – not so loud this time – and another step or two, and he was right inside a large hallway with a grand staircase ahead of him.

Now, inside the house, he realised what he hadn't understood all along. It was a magician's house, yes most definitely it was and he felt the house welcoming him home. What he had forgotten was that he was the magician. It was his house all along!

Books by Will Parfitt from PSA Books

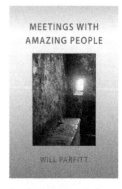

Meetings with Amazing People

Blurring the boundaries between reporting, allegory and fantasy, Will describes an early search for spiritual wisdom and enlightening meetings with an array of amazing people.
'A deligthful and spiritually nourishing read ...this book will settle something in your soul.' [MR]

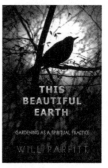

This Beautiful Earth

This book contains many stories that describe a deep perspective on gardening as a spiritual practice. It can connect you to an older archetypal rhythm, the rhythm of nature and the earth herself.
'This lovely little book puts you in touch with the healing nature of the earth and the web that connects everything.' [AR]

The Something and Nothing of Death

Death is present through life and the more we face this truth, the more death becomes a wise advisor encouraging us to live life more fully.
'A straight-forward and compassionate journey ... asnyone of any faith or none could read this and feel a congruence... a superb achievement.' [MR]

The Magic of Psychosynthesis

Psychosynthesis is an ideal system for deep inner exploration and magical development. Explore your connection to Will, Imagination and Love, the essential components for your personal and spiritual growth.

'This book is clearly a labour of love. If you are interested in understanding more about the mystery of our spiritual nature...this is a book to read.' [KS]

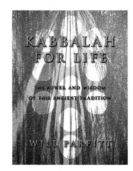

Kabbalah For Life

This book explores this fascinating and ancient tradition and how relevant it is to our everyday lives. With practice, Kabbalah deepens our connection to life and to our underlying spiritual journey.

'Ancient, wonderful, deep, foreboding and magical all at the same time.' [LT]

For details of these and other books
by Will Parfitt visit

www.willparfitt.com

available from Amazon
amd to order from all good bookshops

Kindle editions also available

Printed in Great Britain
by Amazon